Motherish

Motherish

stories by
Laura Rock Gaughan

TURNSTONE PRESS

Motherish
copyright © Laura Rock Gaughan 2018

Turnstone Press
Artspace Building
206-100 Arthur Street
Winnipeg, MB
R3B 1H3 Canada
www.TurnstonePress.com

Turnstone Press gratefully acknowledges the assistance of the Canada Council for the Arts, the Manitoba Arts Council, the Government of Canada through the Canada Book Fund, and the Province of Manitoba through the Book Publishing Tax Credit and the Book Publisher Marketing Assistance Program.

Cover photograph: Shutterstock 579250834

Printed and bound by Friesens in Canada.

Library and Archives Canada Cataloguing in Publication

Gaughan, Laura Rock, 1964-, author
    Motherish / Laura Rock Gaughan.

Short stories.
Issued in print and electronic formats.
ISBN 978-0-88801-641-6 (softcover).--ISBN 978-0-88801-642-3 (EPUB).--ISBN 978-0-88801-644-7 (PDF).--ISBN 978-0-88801-643-0 (Kindle)

    I. Title.

PS8613.A9365M68 2018   C813'.6   C2018-902848-3
                                                C2018-902849-1

Canada Council   Conseil des arts
for the Arts   du Canada

MANITOBA ARTS COUNCIL
CONSEIL DES ARTS DU MANITOBA

Funded by the Government of Canada
Financé par le gouvernement du Canada   Canada   Manitoba

for Tim

Contents

Motherish

Good-Enough Mothers

 tella pushes hills of spaghetti around her plate, pretending she hasn't heard me. Her fork flattens the hills into tomato-red mudslides. She checks to see if Hazel, finger painting with her own spaghetti and sauce in the high chair, is watching the destruction.

Standing at the sink, elbow-deep in water filled with last night's dishes, I try again. "Lunchtime's over. Back to school!"

It's hard to find a fresh approach to her resistance. I refuse to become one of those counting-out-loud mothers who turn power struggles with their kids into inescapable performance art. The plates clatter as I toss them, still dripping soap, into the drainer.

"Stella, really. Wash your hands and put your jacket on."

Hazel whines, her face flushed. She squirms against the high chair's seat belt, batting the food-slick tray, as her whine gains force and altitude before resolving into rhythmic shrieking.

"I'm warning you," I singsong. "That's a lethal frequency stabbing my brain."

I'll be like one of those pithed frogs in high school bio lab. What will happen to this family if Mama Judy gets pithed? And immediately I cross-examine myself—Barbara's out of town, but I can still play her part. Don't you realize, Judy, that the child's only six; why should she be governed by *your* schedule? And toddlers whine, don't you know that by now? That's what they do. Yes, ma'am, I certainly do know that.

Mt. Hazel erupts again.

"Oh, what is it, baby?" I reach for a wet cloth and pause. Green-tinged ropes of snot hang from Hazel's nostrils, one side longer and edging past the upper lip. Onset of the cold Stella just kicked.

Such a bad night: up to comfort Hazel, and then Stella woke with a nightmare, which I'm blaming on the tow-truck guys. They come and go at all hours, never failing to rev their engines. Their flashers circle the front bedroom, illuminating our private space, Barbara's and mine. When she's here, Barbara almost always sleeps through it while I lie awake and think of fatal accidents, flipping my pillow, tensing at every sound. It makes me want to move, even though Barbara talked us into this neighbourhood. The East End: easy commute downtown, short walk to the Beaches but not as pricey; family-oriented yet gritty; a still-real place that's rough in patches.

Barbara missed last night. She's away on business again, law conference spanning the bloody weekend, which matters not at all to her firm, but aggrieved life partners beg to differ. And so it's double-double mother trouble for me. I'm not TGIFing much, over here. Still, I do my best not to resent her mobility, to welcome her home again and again.

Bits of pasta decorate Hazel's hair, the high-chair tray, and the floor. I touch a clean spot on her forehead—she feels warm, but normal warm or sick? Hazel grunts, and the smell of a filled diaper mixes with lunch.

"Stinky," Stella says, holding her nose. She still hasn't moved from the table.

Stella doesn't want to go back to school because she's jealous of the baby at home with me. Here in Paradise. I yank the plate from her and place it in the sink. Drop the cloth and lift Hazel out of the chair, keeping the tray from falling with one knee, and hold her at arm's length. "Get. Your. Jacket. On."

Parenting books don't talk about times like this, when you're divided. Stella needs to be walked to school; Hazel needs a bath—just the type of situation that would send Barbara running to the liquor cabinet. Imagine her on duty instead of me; imagine, also, a newborn alongside Stella and Hazel. It is to laugh. She couldn't cope, not for one school lunch hour.

I wrap Hazel in a blanket, arranging it to cover the yuck. With one hand, I fasten Stella's buttons and nudge her, not gently, outside. The school is close, but we're late every day.

Fatima waits on the sidewalk at the border of our yards. I suspect she won't judge me for my filthy baby or any number of maternal failings. She waves at Stella and gives me a wry half-smile. "I'll walk her over, Judy," she says in that loud voice, stripped of intonation, and watches my face. Fatima doesn't sign, she reads lips.

"Would you?" I flip the blanket to show her Hazel's hair sticky with tomato sauce, and she steps back, grimacing. I lean down to kiss Stella, who's now eager to go—with anyone but me?—and watch them walk hand-in-hand, past the forsythia hedge at the corner, with its fresh green leaves, not yet ready to bloom. When I can no longer see them, I slump against the gatepost, switching Hazel to my other hip. What do I really know about Fatima? Recently, I've begun streetproofing Stella: scream if a stranger grabs you; never agree to help find the lost puppy, there *is* no puppy; what would you do if …? What would you do if the seemingly harmless neighbour, thirtyish, single, childless, afflicted with an aura of deep sorrow, turns out to be a baby killer? But this is sleep deprivation. I never used to be terrified all the time. Now, even good days, I'm plagued by uncertainty. My constant question, only half ironic: What Would a Good Mother Do? WWAGMD—gag reflex. Unanswerable question, because what is this mythical creature, the good mother? First it is necessary to find one.

After school, I watch the tow-truck antics, the daily spectacle. The girls are plugged into a TV show upstairs; *Dora the Explorer*'s electro-synth voice and Hazel's babbled responses provide periodic sound checks. Stella, old enough to know Dora won't converse, giggles.

One of the guys reverses the truck to loud warning beeps. His brother stands on the sidewalk, waving his arm: keep her coming, c'mon, c'mon, up shoots the hand. The driver hops out. Standing by the rear wheels, they begin the routine. First, they disassemble the towing rig, removing metal pieces the size of arms and legs, wiping them with oily rags before fastening them into place again. Next, they open the doors and pull out candy wrappers and cigarette packs, foam coffee cups, beer cans, dropping them on the ground. Once, as a grand finale, the driver pissed in the gutter, standing by the truck with his back to me, swaying, while his brother hooted.

From her front porch next door, Fatima watches them too. This is a promising avenue of conversation; many a new friendship has blossomed in the heat of shared contempt. I'll have to ask her about them.

The back window of the truck's cab is covered by a large decal, a stylized black rose. I noticed it walking home from the store one day, pushing Hazel in the stroller, my urban barge. Beneath the rose, a line of script reads IN MEMORY OF JACK 1994 TO 2012. Who is this Jack? Was there another brother who no longer walks (and spits and swears and throws garbage) among us? Every time I study this clue I try to muster some empathy but fail. Any generous impulses that I once possessed have been driven away by nocturnal masculine banter. Laugh, shout, peel away from curb, repeat.

"Look," I said to Hazel, pointing at the rose, "a mobile memorial. How touching. How very tasteful." She fussed, probably irked by the biscuit boxes wedged around her, and began to bawl. "A vehicular tattoo. Grief on wheels. Yes, cry! You've got the right idea. My brilliant baby."

They're boys, really. Barbara thinks they're hilarious, says we should have them over for drinks. Right! Come into our lesbian lair, young hetero lads. Bring your teen girlfriends, the waifs with incurious black-rimmed eyes. As they spar, night after night, in their front yard, I'm stuck ringside. Surely I know more about them than they know about me—if they've even registered my constant presence in the home opposite theirs.

Sometimes they discuss their competition.

"It's war," one of the tow-boys said to friends gathered around their front stoop on a midsummer's eve when sleep eluded me, as it so often does. "Those Chinese Chink companies, they're buying all the rigs, making everyone work for them. But let's be honest, we'll always beat 'em to the scene."

His brother answered, "Don't say Chink like that," and I sat up in bed, hopeful. "Chink *means* Chinese," he continued. "Don't say Chinese Chink, just pick one."

I lay back, soul-tired. The only time I ever called a tow truck, a fat, balding white guy showed up. But of course I'm no expert on the towing industry. And the boys must be, because they're always out on the road, waiting for an accident to happen so they can go to work.

Fatima and her mother, Nilda, brought their shaggy dog over to meet us before we moved in. We were waiting for the movers to arrive with our furniture, so all we had in the house were delicate things—boxes of china and Barbara's collection of paintings, stacked against the wall. The dog galumphed around the room, stopping at the canvases to sniff them. Barbara stepped between the animal and the art, pretending to make friends.

"Cookie looks menacing," Nilda said, "but she's harmless. A slobbery mushball." Had I known more about her then, I would have realized that Nilda was not as she presented herself. She looked harmless, vaguely warm and motherish, but in reality, capable of doing damage. She put her face next to the dog's muzzle. "Yes, you're a mushball. Aren't you, Cookie, aren't you?"

Nilda's an artist, but not the anything-goes-I'm-open-to-it kind of artist. I saw her face twitch when she did the math on our little family, Barbara and Stella and me, heavily pregnant, still two months away from delivering Hazel.

They stayed just long enough for Nilda's information dump: the artist's life! Disappearing into foreign landscapes to paint! The global witnessing she is called to do! With Fatima's infirmities, it's a comfort having good neighbours; everyone looks out for everyone else on this street.

Fatima followed Nilda's lips and never blinked. She didn't react when her mother yammered her private disease details—dialysis twice a week and languishing on the kidney transplant waiting list, also diabetic, also deaf from a childhood fever. Nilda didn't respond when Barbara said, as she took Stella's hand and together they pet the dog, "Our daughter's going to love it here." Then she came over and placed a hand on my belly, saying, "Both kids, of course. We're all going to love this place." And still the mother said nothing, just flipped paintings.

Barbara wishes I'd quit obsessing. Find some mother-friends, relax with our kids as we swap tales. And she wants another baby, unbelievably. I felt like an old first-time mother at thirty-six. Now I'm really old, judging by the playground, where the other moms bore me with their talk of preserving produce from their tiny urban gardens—canning, of all the time-sucking throwbacks a woman could give in to. They knit and practise yoga and mindful parenting and blog about it all. I thought maturity would give me an edge over the young moms, but I'm always tired. And never certain about what to do. I worry about the psychic state of a six-year-old forced back to school after the lunch recess—will she need counselling? I ponder the precedent set by a lollipop, the artificial ingredients therein, whether it is a more or less acceptable treat if consumed in front of the television. Other worries: drowning, freak accidents, meningitis. But my biggest fear is that the one thing I forget to be afraid of, some tiny, overlooked detail, is what will get us in the end.

Where is the certainty that my mother and her card-playing, cocktail-swilling girlfriends displayed? Maybe my question should be What Would a Good-Enough Mother Do? Somehow, I manage, though. Better than Barbara would. Much as I love her, honesty compels me to state that fact. She couldn't be the mother I am.

Two, we agreed. Two was enough, our family finished. Three would require too many ketchupy meals, years more diapers and diarrhea, peanut butter streaks on walls. More joy, too, I'll admit that. More love.

Well, why shouldn't we have another baby? Because clearly I'm coping so well. And she wants it all, Barbara does. Me at home with a growing brood, and me keeping up appearances, and me working, too. Her expectations always unmet.

"You should find a part-time gig, or maybe freelance," Barbara said as we set the table one evening last month. "Something you can manage through pregnancy."

I had prepared a special meal for her homecoming, deferred until after the youngsters' bedtime: seared scallops, long-simmering risotto with mushrooms, chocolate mousse, good wine. Our conversation had been carefully upbeat at first, but after a few drinks Barbara was ready to negotiate. She was home only overnight, the next day flying to Vancouver for a week-long huddle with her western legal team. "You've missed work, Judy. Anyone can see you're not taking care of yourself."

I paused on the threshold of the kitchen to decode this. She meant unwashed hair days. Frayed, sweat-stained shirts. I repelled her.

"Big wide world, remember? Seems like you have cabin fever."

"I believe I'm fully engaged. Being their mother is a full-time job. You'd know that if you were ever here."

"That's an interesting position to take," Barbara said, leaving her dishes on the counter, not even rinsing them.

"Don't be like that," I said, but we were done. Later, sliding into bed after Barbara was asleep, I snuggled into the solidity of her spine and mapped the depressions of her vertebrae with one finger. Mouth open, she whistled softly with each exhalation, like a siren receding. An alarm sounding repeatedly as I lay awake thinking about how I would muster the energy to carry another baby.

Fatima and I mostly wave. After walking Stella to school, she gives me a thumbs-up on her way back home. From my watchpost at the front window, I gesture *namaste* in return.

Sometimes we chat in our front yards—she, engaged in desultory raking; me, following the kids around, picking up Hazel

when she falls and setting her on the path, where she can practise her beginner steps—and Fatima fills me in. Her parents
were divorced when she was young; her father lives in the Junc-
tion. He comes to see her when Nilda goes away, mornings after
his night shift ends. She once held a job in a mailroom but was
forced to leave because dialysis took too much time. She doesn't
go out, and no friends come in, as far as I can see.

The look of longing on her face. It's there when she shuffles
past and when she sits on her porch, tapping cigarette ash into
her palm, tracking the tow-boys. I imagine she thinks I have it
all: a loving partner and kids. Perhaps there's no particularity
to her longing, though; maybe she just doesn't want to be stuck
in her own frail life anymore. Even the tow-girlfriends have a
better deal.

Whenever her mother travels, I say, "Just ask if you need anything; I'm next door." She can't phone, she doesn't email, but she
does have a fax machine. Barbara's home office has a fax, so we
send missives back and forth, something I'd almost forgotten
how to do. Obsolete professionals are full of useless knowledge.
When insomnia hits, I head down to the basement to work on a
freelance article, my re-entry ticket to paid work and a fulfilled
partner, although I'm taking my sweet time on that. Then the
phone rings and clicks, receiving data, and the printer disgorges
Fatima's sadness. I craft brief domestic narratives in reply—
Stella's swimming lessons, a new milestone for Hazel. I'm here
for this exchange, but for a limited time only, given how busy I
obviously am.

The tow-boys are champion sperm producers. Both girlfriends
got pregnant, but then one disappeared. Through the winter I
watched the girl who stayed. Her belly popped from her boy-
ishly thin frame, poking out of her unzipped parka, yet I noticed

11

she was able to wear her regular jeans until the last month, when she switched to leggings. No stretchy maternity panels for that one. Her eyes seemed to grow larger too, or else she was doing extra rounds with the eyeliner. She moved heavily between their house, with its sagging porch and missing shutter on the first-floor window, and the boys in their shiny truck, bringing them beer as they played cards.

The idea of these kids having kids. One night when they were definitely away, I scurried across the street and left my pregnancy manual on the porch. That girl needs help. Not that she'll take it. I keep checking, though. The book is gone, but I've never seen her reading it.

A couple weeks ago I realized that she hadn't been around for a while, and then she returned, perfectly skinny, clutching her new responsibility. Now, she paces up and down the sidewalk and back into the house, her circumscribed perimeter. I haven't seen the baby's face, just swaddled blankets. The kid—the mother!—looks fourteen. Father tow-boy barely glances at her or the baby. Something unpredictable has grown between them. Nerves, accusation.

The other afternoon, Stella stood next to the rocker as I nursed Hazel. Soon I'll have to think about weaning, but not yet. The tugging at my breast, the flaming arrow to the groin as my milk let down and I settled into the task, unvalued by the working world yet indisputably necessary. I gazed at Hazel's damp cheek, her face scrunched in concentration, put an arm around Stella, and pulled her close, and we made a tight trio. Stella told me her class was learning about things to be when you grow up. Careers, essentially. A word I can no longer pronounce without sneer quotes. Because I've chopped my career into tiny pieces? Because careerism is a dangerous illusion? I wanted to warn

Stella that a career will never love you, but I stopped myself. She freed herself from my grasp and began hopping on one foot.

"The teacher says I can be a fireman, or a nurse, or a chef, or actually anything," she said, panting. I smile at *actually*. My bright girl. She came back to the chair and peered into my face. "How did you decide to be nothing?"

How indeed? I should send that one to a magazine. As an editor, I took satisfaction in wrestling with other people's words. A job too abstract for a child to understand—no uniform, I get that. I'm still laughing with my darling. And yet. I didn't expect to be undone by the relentless need for my attention. I wasn't a baby person before, but now I am. I regularly bore friends, former colleagues, and my lover.

Fatima seemed fine earlier, but she's sick again. This evening, as I was folding laundry, she sent a fax saying, 'Fell out of bed, what a clumsy oaf! Not a good day, after all.'

I quickly fax back, 'Crazy busy over here. Never a dull moment. But can I get you anything?'

Five minutes later, the incoming fax arrives. She needs milk. I curse Nilda, wherever she is. So she has a problem with our nuclear family configuration. Well, I have a problem with her free-spirit flights. She should try painting our neighbourhood; there's plenty of life to witness right here.

The fight has already started across the road, and it's getting louder. A few extra guys hang with the tow-boys tonight. I check on the kids, grab my wallet, lock myself out, and *run* into the chilly dark. I've never left them home alone before. It's not far to the corner store, but all the way I'm thinking headlines and jail time and public shame. What if there's a fire? How long does it take for flames to spread in the old, close-set buildings on this street? Minutes, and I'd be out on the sidewalk. And Barbara away yet again. I almost fall to my knees.

I buy the milk and stop at Fatima's, try the door: unlocked. I call out and immediately feel foolish. I've never been inside before. The entrance is dark, surrounded by wood-panelled walls dimly visible in the light from a small round window on the landing of the stairs above me. That window jars me—the layout is the same as our place, and so I could climb the stairs and know which way to bedrooms, which to the washroom. I banish the sudden image of Nilda in her bed, waiting for me.

Here I stand, shivering, my kids alone, and where's the dog? What if this is some kind of trap? You read about these mishaps, where the mother intended to return right away, and no one finds the babes for days.

A single light shines at the far end of the hallway. I step in, set the milk at the bottom of the stairs, back away. Run home, unlock my door with unsteady hands, lock it behind me. Charge upstairs to find Stella mumbling in her sleep, words I can't make out. Hazel's breath is deep and even, her face unperturbed. Thankful. Thanks.

I return to the basement to send one last fax, checking off the Fatima obligation: 'Left the milk inside, talk tomorrow. Feel better!'

The fight across the street turns rough. An older guy comes out—father of tow-boys?—and starts yelling. Then the girl-friend appears—where's the baby?—and pushes her man in the chest, shrieking. Soon they're wrestling on the front lawn. The guys cheer them on.

I cannot leave the window, must monitor the brawl. Should I call the police? Maybe someone else will call. Where is that baby? The older guy slowly sets his beer down and steps, unsteadily, between them. The girlfriend keeps coming, and he shakes her until she howls. The fighting's never lasted this long. Poor babe. I hope it's sound asleep. Noise doesn't penetrate an infant's skin the way it does mine. After a long time at the window, I finally go to bed, only to thrash fitfully, mired in dreams requiring me to be constantly vigilant.

First light Saturday morning, a banging door wakes me. I stagger outside in my bathrobe to pick up the paper. The girlfriend stands across the way, hands on hips, surveying plastic milk crates filled with clothing, a line on the sidewalk. She glances over but doesn't acknowledge me. Her lips are pursed, eyes puffy and red, and for once not edged in black, so she looks even younger than she is. Skin so pale: probably anemic. She doesn't appear to be strong enough for any more drama, but she slams the door going in and out.

I hope my babies stay in bed. Sometimes they'll wake but not get up, chattering in their high voices, bed to crib to bed, and I'll realize anew how lucky I am to hear their emergent conversations. Sometimes I want to hand Hazel to Fatima, give her a temporary fix of that life force, pure hope. I make tea, check on the progress outside. Only six. Her material possessions in six crates.

The doorbell rings, jolting me to the entrance. CHILDREN SLEEPING, I want to shout. I open up warily, jamming my foot behind the door, to a skinny man standing on the porch. There's something familiar about his sloping shoulders. He's older but ageless—fifty or seventy, impossible to tell. He clears his throat, introduces himself as Fatima's father, no name given. I look frankly into his face and identify her long nose and dark eyes. I pull my robe tighter, cross my arms.

"I must you to tell." He pauses, examining his shoes.

He's originally from Portugal, I knew that. Fatima told me

the story of how he met Nilda, whose family is from the same village, while she was an exchange student in Lisbon. Long ago.

"I feel it much to disturb this house."

I clutch the doorknob, mind running ahead to fill in the blank of this news: Barbara? No, that makes no sense. Nilda?

"My daughter, she die." His voice cracks at the end. He looks up at the ceiling of our verandah. "Night passada."

I fall back, hand over throat. His fingers cup his cheeks: he looks stricken, but also embarrassed to have to convey the bluntest of facts: shock strangled by propriety. I mouth *sorrysorrysorry*. A soundtrack in my head instructs me to invite him in, offer tea and sympathy. And somehow, I can't. I don't even know this man. There are babies to protect. How can I be sure it's true? I see everything in this neighbourhood; I keep watch. He conned his way in, people will say later, and murdered the children in their beds.

And why did he come to me? As soon as the question arises, I know. My faxed pages—I see them, falling to the floor of the darkened house next door—have brought him. My breezy notes, the last received or not received. I can't probe for details about her final moments. Poor Fatima. Before or after the milk delivery? I will never be able to ask this.

His face betrays nothing further. I waver, mute, inadequate to this crisis. Finally he nods, walks through our gate, turns down Fatima's walk, and enters her house.

Creeping into the girls' room, I cup Hazel's head in my hand and then crawl into bed with Stella. She turns over, presses her back into my front. A parent has lost a child. An adult child, sickly, but neither of those things would alter the magnitude of loss. Fatima, my semi-friend, my cipher: I didn't really try to understand you.

Morning doesn't officially begin until the kids are up, but I pour cereal into plastic bowls, screw lids on sippy cups. I won't tell them anything when they come for breakfast, not yet. God, how am I supposed to explain death to either one of them? If only Barbara were here. Why am I the one who has to handle everything? Would she come home early if I called?

More noise: the clanking, chiming tow truck. I march to the window. Those people are hopeless. Both tow-boys loiter on the sidewalk, the baby's father bearing a black eye. He puts on dark glasses, gets in, and runs the damned truck, imperceptibly adjusting its angle against the curb, honks the horn, gets out. They curse. Chocolate bars are opened, wrappers tossed on the ground; gloved hands test the winch. The brother steps into the street, reaches in the open driver-side window, and honks the horn. The girl comes out, hair in a raggedy bun, carrying the baby. Her crates are gone. They're still arguing, she from the porch, the two boys at the street. The hem of the baby's blanket drags on the ground in front of her as she crosses the yard. Don't trip. Don't. She says something unintelligible. Her boyfriend shrugs, walks around to the passenger door, and opens it. She hands him the bundle, and I cringe. Don't. He holds the baby in one arm and helps her into the cab with the other. Then he lifts it up to her and closes them in. I look at her profile, curled over the child, rocking gently. Wait for her to find the car seat and settle the baby in it, but she doesn't. Wait for her to wrap a seatbelt around herself, at least, but she doesn't. I automatically look toward Fatima's house—does she see this?—and then correct myself. No, she doesn't.

Father tow-boy gets into the truck, guns the motor, and takes off. The boy left behind stands on the sidewalk, appearing uneasy and naked without his rig. He watches the truck turn at the intersection, then studies our house. He meets my gaze with a defiant stare before going back inside. I snap the curtains closed. Check on my babies upstairs, who are chanting a verse about chirping birds, and return to the living room, to my post by the window. I wonder if funeral arrangements are being made at this moment by Fatima's father, if he'll call Nilda overseas and tell her to come home, and if he'll say why, or if he'll wait until she arrives. Which would be worse? There are no good options for the absent mother.

Should I have phoned an ambulance last night? Would Fatima be alive if I'd done that? Was it even her illness? I can't shake the idea that she chose death. What if I'd gone into the house all the way? What was the right thing to do? It's too late for doubt—so futile and fleeting, so quick to dissolve into a thin wash of grief. Fatima, the observer who did not judge, who had no skin in the complex, competitive games of motherhood: gone in an instant.

I circle the living room, searching for the notebook where, long ago, I wrote the licence number of the tow truck. Lift cushions off the couch, check underneath. Dizzy with questions. Sick about an infant unsecured in a speeding vehicle. Stupid kids, inexplicably entrusted with life. Perhaps they'll lose custody; perhaps the kiddie-parents will be forced to attend training camp. That's not my problem.

Finally, I find it—Stella has doodled over the numbers, an angel-winged stick figure that makes me smile even in my state—and thankfully she hasn't drawn a house on fire. My daughter has a shot at being well adjusted. The number is legible under the crayon. I pick up the phone. This is a day of decision, a day that's about to get much worse for certain people.

But then I stop myself, hearing Barbara's voice parodying this act. How typical of you, she'll say, to think calling the cops is a decisive action. You might feel better, but it will make no difference in the long run to the baby, my darling. We don't get to choose our parents. Who do you think you are, the baby-fixer?

My hand hovers mid-air. It's hard enough to win arguments with Barbara when she's here.

The truck screeches to a halt out front. The girlfriend sets her bundle on the seat. He gets out first. She leaves the truck door ajar, encroaching on the sidewalk that earlier displayed her belongings. Together, the parents walk into the house. Carrying nothing.

I step onto the verandah, check up and down the street. No one around. It's still early, and I remember: Saturday. My bathrobe covers me to the ankles; my slippers are moccasins, good enough. Hiking the robe, I run across the road, reach the safety of the truck, and crouch down on the street side. Quickly I open the door, lean into the cab, and slide the blankets toward me, across the gleaming slab of bench seat. A mewl, and then a slight movement that might have been imagined, as I shift the weight into my arms. Backing out of the truck, I'm already rocking gently.

Six paces and we're safe inside. I unwrap the bundle on the couch, inspecting: a little girl. She looks well fed—the right amount of fat ringing her wrists and upper thighs, the feet plump and pink. Infant smell surrounds her: sour milk and warm scalp and soap. I nuzzle her neck, breathing deeply. Freed from the blankets, she flails her limbs, yet meets my eyes placidly, unblinking blueness. Her peaceful new soul offers reassurance: you did the right thing, Judy. See? No crying. *You* are the good mother. You know what to do.

Only I don't. Trembling, I rewrap the baby and hold her close. If there were bruises or signs of malnourishment, no one would condemn this theft.

The baby sighs, settles into sleep, and her body quells my shakes. We walk, hovering at the edge of the window, out of the sight of passersby. I hum tunelessly.

"Mama, I want a snack," Stella calls down the stairs, stopping my walk mid-stride, striking me dumb. I clear my throat.

"Just a minute, honey," I whisper. While I take care of this usurper, alright? And you and your sister and this newborn and I will all live here undisturbed, happily ever freaking after. My breathing is audible, harsh recrimination.

"Mama?"

"Hang on, Stella! Be there in a sec!"

I look around for something to give the baby. Yes. I will construct a rationale, gild it with gifts. Here are items we no longer need, because Hazel outgrew them. We're finished having children, you see. The narrative builds itself.

With one hand, I reach into the storage trunk that doubles as a coffee table, where I'd been stashing supplies just in case. A few outfits, a package of disposable diapers, some Q-tips and ointment. A baby-wipe warmer, forgotten shower gift, the most useless item known to woman, but this is about making a gesture. Everything must go.

I fill a shopping bag. A small teddy bear peeks over the top, anchored by pink receiving blankets, never used. I shift the baby upright, pick up the bag, and prepare my announcement: impromptu baby shower—surprise! But I'm too late for guilt offerings.

The couple re-emerges. I'm counting down steps and seconds until they reach the truck, and when they do, the mother cries out. The tow-boy doesn't react. Shocked into blankness or dulled by his hangover.

They look under the truck, walk around it. The girl sinks to the curb, hugging her knees. Her shoulders slump. Even now, holding her infant, I want to snap at her to remove her feet from the road before someone runs them over.

The boy pulls out his phone, looks at it. His brother comes out, says something, and they all look across the street, at my house. I'm sure they can't see me, but I fall back from the window anyway. No one makes a move.

For a breath or two, I think they might be entertaining the idea of doing nothing. As though they could just walk away and call this an even exchange: their kid for getting their freedom back, escaping the drudgery of playing house. A silent sob catches my throat, sorrow for their plight and possibly mine. Home looks very different from inside and out. I imagine they see it as a trap rather than a haven, and I can understand that. They remain suspended, until the girl's face crumples. She wails, for real this time—body heaving, head on knees. The boy shakes his head, bends over the phone.

I caress the baby's face, which reveals no likeness to either parent. A face suffused with contentedness, singularly devoted to sleeping. I feel stored energy beneath the blankets and think of transferring some of it to Fatima. If only she could have held her. Maybe she did. Not everything occurs within sight of my window.

Three decisive strides to the door, carrying the baby and her shopping bag on a gust of goodwill: that's what it will take to restore everyone's sanity. I can make that trip, smile glued on, bearing gifts, full of chatter about neighbours looking after each other—and isn't that, when all is said and done, what makes this street so great? What the good-enough mother will do, this time. Return the baby to fate.

Maquila Bird

Maru reached for another jacket and draped it across the sewing table. Before starting, she took a moment to adjust the plastic specimen bottle strapped to her belly. It was warm, a comfort against tender skin. She revved her machine and guided the garment to the pouncing needle. As the quality control tag—Made by/Hecho por 867—met the needle plate, she inserted a different tag behind it and finished the seam. It took the merest flick of a finger; no one saw her do it. Where would her handiwork end up? Perhaps a tall and loud American girl in New York or LA would sling Maru's creation over her shoulder for a winning look. She liked to think so. Daydreaming a life for the girl, she imagined a family, an admiring beau, and a clutch of stylish friends, who all found reason to admire the girl's jacket, even if they didn't go so far as to wonder about the unseen person who had made it.

Pukka-pukka-pukka filled the room and her head and her bones. It was the sound of steel puncturing denim, Maru's first stitch tracking to infinity, joining the stitches of a thousand other workers. They sat in numbered rows in the harshly lit hangar of an abandoned airfield on the outskirts of Tijuana. Today it was jean jackets, but not always. Sometimes they made lingerie, and, other times, stretchy outfits for yoga, tennis, or jogging, clothes good for only one thing.

The workers had clothes for just one thing: working. Dress code was a loose pink smock and matching surgical cap. Management was strict about hair; Señor Ramos inspected for flyaway wisps during the mandatory team cheer that began each day. *Pride in our product and homeland; excellence second to none.* During break, Maru and her friends returned to the topic of his hair obsession as if adding another patch to a quilt they were fashioning together.

"Regulations, maybe," she said.

"Yes, it's for sanitation," said Juanita. "I believe that's the reason." She echoed Maru loyally, yet sounded independent, more like the spirited ally she used to be before Maru's brother, Adalberto, had stolen her thoughts.

"We're not making food," Lucinda said. "Or medicine." She struck a match and lit her cigarette, sucking hard.

Rosita snorted. "It's so he can look at your neck, obviously. Sicko." She tapped her ash onto the weathered picnic table, where they sat during breaks. Beneath the table, a growing pile of butts reminded Maru of the white-tipped buds of the sole plant in the packed dirt yard, a manzanita branching across the rusty fence, continually setting blossoms only to drop them before they could flower.

"But the uniforms—it's nice not to worry about what to wear each day," Maru said, ticking the reasons on her fingers. "If you fall behind, they don't know immediately who it is. And it's something we share, isn't it? It shows we're all sisters here."

"Oh, I was waiting for this," Rosita said. She groaned. "Maria Eugenia. Maru-baby. You love this dump so much? Is that why you're always singing? You do realize that over there"—she pointed north, toward the border—"they gain in one hour what we make working all day."

"What can we do?" Juanita said. "There is much we cannot change." She bestowed a sad smile of resignation on Maru, who suffered Adalberto's absence with her, if not so acutely.

Rosita exhaled a stream of smoke. "There will be no change as long as we do nothing. Think about it: they will need us even more in the time of free trade than they did before."

Rosita kept them informed about the twists and turns of the North American treaty, whether they were interested or not. It was the reason so many new maquiladoras were springing up, she said, and it represented an opportunity, if the workers could just figure out how to express themselves through strong action.

Maru shrugged. This side or that, she didn't envy anyone. She hugged herself and felt, beneath the smock, her golden treasure. It sloshed with every movement. She was probably the only one who could hear it, but she'd been pretend-coughing whenever the machines stopped, wanting to fill the sudden void with a sound more definite than the ringing in her ears and the buzzing of the gigantic lights mounted overhead.

Her lips twitched. Smuggling something as disgusting as urine into the plant was hilarious. Only Juanita knew, for it was she who had donated the precious fluid that was going to get Maru through test day. If she flunked the test, she'd be marched out of the building and replaced by another girl from the perpetual lineup of applicants. Rosita's sister had been terminated in just this way, so the company could avoid paying motherhood benefits. Soon enough, she wouldn't be able to hide the pregnancy, but until then she intended to keep her income. Even though her plan was to leave this place, she wanted the leaving to be on her own terms. She still needed to save money.

And she still had to convince her husband that her new dream was worth following—the adventure that would carry them far from here. And that meant, for now, concealing her condition from the bosses.

Señor Ramos appeared on the other side of the fence, pacing. They took their time standing up. Rosita cursed under her breath and ground her cigarette into the dirt.

Maru was delayed by her need for the bathroom, so she was alone when Señor Ramos stopped her. They stood just inside the shop door, which was left open to catch a non-existent breeze. She stepped back, but he held her arm with moist hands, forcing her closer. He didn't accord her the respect due to a married woman.

"Tough times ahead"—he checked her name tag—"Maria Eugenia." He scanned the cloudless horizon of the industrial park as if taking in the nightly business news while she waited, wondering where she might find thread to match the thin blue-washed-over-grey sky. "We find ourselves in a surplus employee situation," he continued. "Definitely, no syndicates are needed here. Take care, my dear. Little gatherings turn quickly into nefarious activities."

"Señor?" Maru reclaimed her arm and corrected the distance between them.

"Ladies chatting might be swapping recipes or they might be holding undesirable meetings; how am I to know? But you're a team player, I'm sure. Listen, I'm doing you a favour by telling you." He leaned in and sniffed deeply. "Is that perfume?"

Maru focussed her gaze on the open collar of his guayabera and spoke softly to his wattles. "Señor, we talk only of church. You yourself would be most welcome at our services—even my husband and brother like to go." She flushed at this bit of embroidery: Hector refused to attend church on the grounds that he was allergic to bullshit, and Adalberto had just gone away again. She and Juanita were the churchgoers. Just two nights ago, they attended services at the new storefront place, Congregación del Buen Pastor, for the first time. Everyone called each other Sister or Brother there. It was a simple whitewashed space with folding chairs, so unlike the gilded, incensed cathedral where Maru, the few times she'd ventured in, never dared to open her mouth in prayer or song. On Wednesday night, she sang like a goldfinch and flew home with a light heart.

Señor Ramos lifted her chin, forcing her to look at his pale, plump face, which struck Maru as babyish for a man of his age and position. "Church, is it?" he said, as she held her breath. "I suggest that you girls watch yourselves."

A week had passed since Adalberto's latest departure. He worked on a picking crew that rolled north with the hot weather. Maru knew better than to hope for a letter from her brother during the long months of his absence. Any news would have to come from Juanita, her almost-sister-in-law; *she* would receive phone calls, but Maru didn't begrudge desperate lovers. If only Juanita would quit her mooning. Just this morning on the bus to work, bouncing over potholes, she'd smoothed Juanita's cheek, gently chiding. "Birds come back, don't they? And butterflies? Everything has its season."

"My Adal-beerrrr-to," Juanita wailed. She opened her mouth to start again, but Maru clapped a hand over her lips and they collapsed in giggles.

Juanita regarded her seriously. "Don't you feel sick, Maru?" She grabbed the seat to steady herself. "This ride makes me want to puke, and I'm not even—"

Maru covered Juanita's mouth again.

"We're here," she said. "Let's sew something beautiful."

Sitting with Hector after supper every evening, Maru transformed the boring quality control tags that she carried home.
Last night, she made bronze suns in the Aztec style, one after
another. She stopped to study her needlework, then pulled the
thread taut and knotted it in back. This sun beamed at her; it
winked as if to say, how sly you are, my creator, how skillful.

Humming a salsa tune—causing Hector to keep time with his
shoulders for a few beats and ask, "Shall we dance, querida?"—
Maru stippled the rays with silver. Practise had paid off. Her
pieces were becoming more intricate, miniature tapestries
showing off the wealth of colour in her mending basket. She'd
been collecting the thread at work; little bits weren't missed.

This design was another joyful variation of her repertoire of
flower-laden hearts, musical notes, rainbows, and stars. Lately,
Maru had been experimenting with stylized patterns that held
no obvious meaning but still made her happy, and that emo-
tion couldn't help but be transmitted to the ultimate owner of
the garment. Her needle went in and out and around the tag
until it was impossible to see the 867—the number of the only
worker who cared enough to customize jackets before they were
baled like hay, loaded into shipping containers, and trucked
northward.

"Why do you bother with those things?" Hector said, flipping
channels to find their telenovela. "This week Luisa is supposed
to find her daughter. You know, she wasn't just kidnapped, she's
also being poisoned. Pay attention to the clues or you'll miss it."

Maru shook her head. "Such a pity men can do only one
thing at a time."

Why bother indeed? She had wondered many times without

reaching a conclusion. Maybe she was driven to make her art in the same way the great Rivera was moved to paint the life of his people on public walls. A vision of herself as Rivera's rightful heir began to take shape; she stared at it through her stitches.

"Ah, mi querida," Hector murmured, leaning his head on her shoulder, "come back to me."

She stopped sewing to stroke his unruly black hair, but she did not come back. From a vantage point above and behind her body, she zoomed out to watch a scene unfold: the magnificent National Palace in the DF—she'd never been to the capital city but recognized the building known to every schoolchild—and beneath its red awnings stood men on either side of a giant painting covered with black cloth. As the painting suddenly stretched taller, the men scaled ladders that appeared as if by magic. They were expectant, waiting for the secret signal to unveil her art to the crowd that had gathered in the Zócalo in order to be among the first to see it. And now it was not a painting, but a two-storey tapestry pinned to cornices, and now a flag rippling in the breeze, hanging from the tallest pole in the city.

"Hola, what planet are you visiting? Are you time-travelling?"

"Shh." She pointed at the TV, playing a montage of Luisa and her extended family in times of crisis and celebration, first young and then older, spooling through past seasons to reach the present one, which held the nation in thrall as the poisoned hostage storyline advanced.

Forget Rivera, maybe she was just a humble graffiti artist, a kid with a can of spray paint who never tired of leaving her mark. Not a star like Luisa or her captured daughter—not a main character at all. There was value in being anonymous, even a kind of freedom. She must be careful not to get caught. That was why she paced herself, inserting only one decorated tag for every thirty or so jackets that she produced. The official tag covered hers completely. Señor Ramos discovering her embellishment was as likely as a camel passing through the eye of a needle.

Her body had not changed on the outside, yet Maru felt different. Her breasts tingled without warning, flashing on and off. In the lower abdomen, nothing definite; some days she couldn't even accept that she was pregnant. But peeing all the time was becoming a problem.

The zone superintendent, an old woman named Teresa, said, "Hija," when Maru asked for the washroom pass. "Again?"

"And what should I do? I have to go."

"Save some for the test. Licenciada Vargas will be here shortly." Teresa gave her the pass.

"Yes, it will soon be our turn to piss in the cup. Good luck, abuelita," Maru said, squeezing Teresa's shoulder as she passed.

"Smart mouth! You're the one who needs it," Teresa called after her.

Squatting in the dingy stall, Maru remembered how she and Hector had planned to wait before starting their family, saving money for the future. Only they weren't planners by nature, and eventually she persuaded him not to decide at all. "There are hidden gifts in everything," she told him, "to be revealed at the right time." But how was it that she had not yet found the moment to reveal the presence of the baby to Hector?

Maru shook the container and listened to the liquid. She cupped her breasts, marvelling at how heavy and warm they were.

Back at her station, she surveyed her growing pile of completed jackets. Other girls made mistakes or nicked themselves, ruining the product with their blood, but Maru had nimble fingers. She pushed fabric through the thrumming machine, singing against the noise. Today she chose mariachi music. If it weren't for the din, anyone would recognize the tune as an old familiar played by strolling men in plazas across the land. Her friends would tease her again about being a sentimental fool, tell her to give hip hop a try. Well, let them have their fun. She looked around the shop until she could pick Juanita out of the pink crowd. She sat a few rows away, side by side with Rosita, both bent over their machines.

Repetitive motion freed her mind to wander. A worry: Señor Ramos's warning this morning. Though more intimate in tone, it reminded her of his rant last week, when he had stopped production with a shrill whistle and gathered everyone around him. He started making what seemed like a routine announcement— one of their shipments had been rejected, he said in measured tones, because of deficiencies. They would have to work double shifts to replace the order they'd already filled. The girls shuffled side to side, arms folded, as he continued his speech. He touched on the company's past quotas and future goals, analyzing its strengths, weaknesses, opportunities—Free trade! Enormous new markets!—and threats, such as lazy, pathetic girls. His oration shifted to the history of the plant during his twenty-year tenure as manager. He recounted the vision of the founding executive team, of which he had been very proud to be part. The more Señor Ramos rambled, the more agitated he became. "Look how far we've fallen," he shouted, emphasizing the word "fallen" by picking up a steam iron and heaving it at the far wall. Metal struck cinder block with a clang. The audience had not been making any noise to speak of yet became more completely silent after the iron was thrown. It was hard not to turn to inspect the crumbling gash left on the wall, but they faced Señor Ramos steadfastly. "We lose all the profit, do you understand? The customers expect better of us!" He dumped a box of scissors on the floor. His face reddened, and flecks of spit fell on some girls. "What don't they want, those junkie bastard norteamericanos? They're addicted to what we send to their malls! More and more and more, they want." He walked out then, leaving Licenciada Vargas behind to make nice. Her speech, a polished meditation on learning from mistakes, was much shorter.

And now she stood at the front of the room, tapping girls on the shoulder. Under her calculating gaze, Maru finished the placket of a right sleeve and began a left. She looked up once to see Señor Ramos scurry in, whisper in Licenciada Vargas's ear, and be dismissed by her. He was the chief, but the coiffed, high-cheeked head of human resources commanded power of her own.

The test was in progress: the chosen ones filed out to the washroom, where nurses stood by to document illicit pregnancy hormones. After each row, the lady turned on spike heels and studied the workers as if making a big decision. Maru almost burst out laughing. She couldn't wait to tell Hector about this— how stupid the managers thought the workers were. Hmm, she thought sarcastically, who will be next?

Perhaps the test had once been a game of chance, but now it was a spreadsheet like the ones charting zone productivity, updated and hung inside the workers' entrance each month, for all to see. Licenciada Vargas spent five days in a zone; each day she picked every fifth girl; by the end of the week, all were tested. Today was Maru's day. And Juanita's day too. Another hour at most, she estimated, watching the fine lady wrapped in her swooping shawl despite the heat, the tropical-print silk a protective layer between her and them. Waiting was hard, but Maru had a plan. She began to sing a lullaby.

When Adalberto returned every year, it was his custom to talk and talk, in soft, rapid torrents, until he wound down to his normal state of silence. Only then did his tense face relax. She and the rest of the family, cousins, aunts, and uncles, would settle around a bonfire, drinking cold beers, and listen patiently. They, the ones who had been left behind, knew he needed to re-enact for them his days away from home: the harvest of smooth tomatoes and prickly cucumbers, still radiating heat; the calluses on his hands and sweat trickling into his eyes; and the waves of exhaustion crashing over his body after he'd picked a field clean. He described the state of every trailer he'd slept in along the way, including the vermin. "True fact," he said once. "You can tell how far you've travelled by the size of the bugs. The colder the air, the smaller they grow." Sometimes he attended hit-or-miss schools for migrant workers, not for nonsensical math lessons that made his eyes blur, but for the free dinner, and, in one particular rural school, the pretty teacher. When he got to the school, they knew he'd reached the end of his narrative. "You'd like that teacher, Hector," he said, winking, "but I don't know if Maru would like her too much." She slapped his knee as he chugged his drink.

The week before last, as he prepared to leave yet again, Adalberto had surprised her by pulling her aside and saying, "Next year, we go all together. You and Hector will come with me." His tone was urgent. For his part, he'd made the decision and there was nothing else to say.

She held him at arm's length, beaming. "Perhaps we will surprise you," she said, speaking to him but looking at Hector over his shoulder. Hector felt the summons and came to her side. He raised a bottle to salute his brother-in-law's journey.

Walking home, though, Hector scoffed at the invitation. It was a joke. A misbegotten sentiment to ease the separation. She did not disagree, for, before now, she hadn't contemplated leaving their city, the web of relations who were her people and Adalberto's, the job that allowed her mind to wander through brilliant patterns and colours of her future creations as she filled her quotas.

In the days since Adalberto had asked her to come, the idea fluttered in her mind like a scrap of unfinished fabric calling for edging. It was both task and emblem, buoying her spirits at in-between moments of her day, as she reached for the pieces of a pattern to assemble, and as she rode the bus home in near-darkness.

Farm labour was hard, dirty work, Maru knew. It was dangerous over there. But she wouldn't be alone. Their family would grow and prosper—this baby first, and others would surely follow. They'd come home every season.

She and Hector had not yet had a serious discussion about leaving. She needed to settle on the best approach. He was a foreman on his shop floor. Other workers kissed up to him for favours. His rate of pay was higher than hers. But she knew her husband. Soon he'd tire of the assembly line, tapping metal panels into place. His destiny was not to make mini-bar fridges, each the same except for different brand names that he affixed with glue. It was true that Hector's maquiladora was better— clean and new, without textile fibres to cloud the air and darken one's snot on the handkerchief. But he could never be content in a windowless room, timing his movements to match the speed of appliances gliding past him. They should feel the sun on their backs, breathe the outdoor air of freedom.

She had reason to hope he would say yes, just as she was saying a silent yes to their child. She envisioned the three of them next year, in the north, together. A dream made real.

Sewing and singing, singing and sewing: Maru didn't mind repetition. There was a natural rhythm to preparing the garment, stitching seams, snipping threads, inspecting the finished piece, tossing it on the pile, and starting over. Even though Licenciada Vargas loomed closer, she decided the next jacket should receive extra artistry. She reached into her pocket for her embroidered tag, a scarlet parrot, and made the insertion undetected. Immediately, Maru felt compelled to do it again—she fingered the raised stitching on a tag, trying to guess which it was—but disciplined her mind. The time was not right. She knew the reason for this itch. The wonder of it still bubbled inside her.

After the final song at church the other night, she and Juanita had filed into the back for fellowship and food, with a potluck feast spread on tables. The room was packed, Juanita drifted away, and she found herself talking with a Sister Ruth, who helped run Congregación del Buen Pastor. She explained that branches of the neo-Pentecostal church dotted the Eastern Seaboard and, indeed, the globe—their communities were growing. This news made Maru feel safe enough to confide her future migration. "On your journey," Sister Ruth responded, "you'll have friends before you even arrive. They'll be waiting for you everywhere you go."

After they'd eaten and helped wash up, Sister Ruth waved at a bin of clothing and said, "That just came from our community in Atlanta. Donations, all good stuff. Help yourself."

Maru took her turn rummaging in the box, wrinkling her nose with distaste at the thought of hand-me-downs. No matter, everything could be washed. She turned the pile, a jumble of colours and textures, seemingly bottomless. Others were waiting behind her. She could feel their impatience building, and yet she couldn't decide. Finally, she reached in without looking and stirred until her hand brushed a piece of clothing that she knew by touch. Ought to know, but could it be? Unbelieving, she drew out a denim jacket with shaking hands and held it to her lips. She sniffed it and turned it inside out to inspect the seams.

Walking away from the others, she flipped the quality control tag over and found underneath her signature moon and stars.

"Something good?" Juanita called from the queue.

Maru held up the jacket.

"No way!" Juanita gave up her place to come see.

"It's a sign," Maru said.

"Of what?"

"I'm not sure. I sent this out to the world, and the world sent it back to me."

"You better not wear it to work. They'll say you stole it."

Sitting at her station, she thought of all the places the jacket might have travelled without her. There was no return address, no message in the bottle. Yet, she felt that this tangible, wearable sign could be relied upon, that it would sustain her on the trip with Hector and Adalberto. And the jacket fit perfectly, snug against her curves. She had never before tried on a garment she'd made at the factory.

She began to sing the hymn she'd learned at the church with Juanita. Just *la-la-la*; she couldn't remember all the words, but the tune was slow and lilting, old and pure. It seemed like the right song for a miracle, the incandescent miracle of the jacket reuniting with its maker.

A sharp fingernail dug into her shoulder. Her hands flew up and away from the needle for safety, the move she'd trained herself to make in all circumstances. She'd been ready for the test, had looked forward to it, even, but she blushed and stumbled getting up.

Fifteen minutes later, it was over. The specimen bottle was still around her waist, empty. She wordlessly thanked Juanita for her gift. Another month of employment, at least a month, longer if her belly didn't grow too quickly. Enough time for her to put aside some of her income for travel. Hector would be impressed with her foresight; he'd have to agree to go. She stared at Juanita, hoping to share a smile of confirmation that the test had gone well, but Juanita was standing and following Licenciada Vargas out the door.

Shortly before quitting time, Maru was startled by shadows falling over her sewing table. Once again, her hands flew away. She'd been singing in full voice and snapped her mouth shut when she realized that Señor Ramos and Licenciada Vargas were standing behind her.

"Come with us," he said. They walked her to the lockers. Licenciada Vargas carried a box of tissues. A scarlet corner of the silk shawl was wound around the hand that held the box; for a moment, she thought it was a bloody bandage.

"Collect your things," he said. "Unfortunately, this must be your last day."

She laced her fingers and said, "I had hoped that if ever my small interventions were noticed, they'd be seen as unique additions to our clothing. What looks bad can sometimes be revealed as good when the time is right."

The managers looked puzzled. Señor Ramos cleared his throat. His oversized authority seemed to have abandoned him as he faced the two women. Maru found herself more frightened by his sheepish manner than she'd been by his clammy touch or ominous warnings. She wished she hadn't suggested that he go to church, so bold. If it wasn't her embroidered tags, what was the problem? Maybe someone from the maquila had reported Maru for wearing the jean jacket on the street. How she loved the feeling of invincibility the jacket gave her when she slipped it on—she'd been out in public twice wearing it. A jealous co-worker snitching? But that was unlikely. Heat flooded her torso; her scalp began to sweat as she tried to guess what was going on. What she must have done wrong, in her ignorance. A flush crept up her neck, and she put a hand there as if to stop it from spreading. The shame of losing a job, when they needed every peso; Hector's anger when he found out; her thwarted plans. The money she earned was necessary for them to travel; the travel necessary to make more money. They'd certainly need cash for the baby. How stuck they were in needs.

Señor Ramos coughed.

"Maria Eugenia," Licenciada Vargas said, not unkindly. "According to your test results, you—well, you are expecting."

Maru stared at her feet, flooded with confusion. The sample—what had gone wrong? And then, recognizing the truth, she gasped. The lost money vanished from her mind. There was only one fact that mattered. It took all her self-control to keep from whooping, but first she had to deal with these high-class marionettes, who expected her to mourn according to their equations of profit and loss.

Maru nodded decisively: yes, she understood. Yes, yes, she'd sign papers. She grabbed them from Señor Ramos, held her hand out for the pen, and signed with a flourish.

"There," she said, slipping the pink smock off, letting it fall to the floor. "That's that."

Señor Ramos looked like a boy whose mother had given him a tongue-lashing. He stuttered as he said, "If you need to call someone—"

"Goodness, we usually see a few tears," said Licenciada Vargas, shifting the tissue box from one cloth-protected hand to the other.

"I can certainly facilitate a phone call."

"I'm fine, fine," Maru said, waving them off. She crumpled the cap into a ball, releasing her hair to swing freely, and left them standing at the workers' entrance.

Maru nearly danced to the bus stop. That her dismissal was an injustice—of course. That she and Hector would scrape the pot harder, possibly even miss a few meals—no argument. Yet, she couldn't dwell on the bad things that had been revealed. If only she could shout this news of a nephew or niece, companion for her son or daughter—a sibling, almost—but she had to wait for Juanita. Surely, after the test, she was being discarded too. It wouldn't be long before she could kiss Juanita's forehead, but patience was impossible when life was so full of promise. For just a few moments, Maru was the only person who knew the whole story, bitter and sweet. She alone could see the journey unfolding for all of them, far away in the north, together.

Transit

The corner of King and Bay is perfect for certain things: planning an office coup alone or with others; talking into a cellphone while walking briskly to the gym; emerging into sudden sunshine after shopping underground; picketing. It's not a good place for doubt or disability. Especially during evening rush hour, when tower workers are anxious and don't need some loser to step over on their way home. Especially if the evening is in December, and snow is falling in fat flakes that disappear on the overheated sidewalk, leaving it clean and shimmering.

It's as good a place as any to run for the streetcar that will carry you away from the financial district and home to the East End. East of money, your workday, the heartbeat of the country.

Nothing unusual about running for the streetcar. It's rumbling blocks away. You'll make it if you sprint past the glassy acreage of Commerce Court and across Bay Street, assuming the lights go your way. You believe in two types of commuters: those who accept waiting for the next car, staring numbly at the overhead screens flashing across the downtown airspace; and those who run for it. You're a runner. Or, rather, you've always been a runner; the impatience and restlessness that spur commuters to run are not only still within you, they've been amplified by the physical changes taking over your body.

You jog along, clutching your purse, overstuffed briefcase, and shopping bags to your side, holding onto your swollen middle, trying in vain to stop the painful ups and downs. Just past the heating grate, your feet slide out from under, and you glide the rest of the distance like a curling stone.

Falling wasn't part of the plan. In your hometown you could blame black ice; does such a thing exist in the city? You're a hick in the world-class metropolis. A glance at the queue of bankers and lawyers holding their shit together way better than you do confirms it. They turn as one toward the streetcar bearing down. Your left hip hurts where you landed. You envision a continuous slide past the line of black rubber overshoes, your body bumping off the curb and onto the tracks, but you've stopped moving.

You roll awkwardly onto hands and knees and push up. The suede pumps with the cunning faux buckle detail are ruined—no friends to pregnant feet, but you loved them anyway—as are the stockings, new out of the package today. However, you still have your token, and you've made the Queen East streetcar, the direct one. You won't have to wait to transfer, contemplating your inadequacies across the street from Babeland, where neon silhouettes of skinny-busty *Girls!!* pulse the night away. Never mind whether the babes inside were born that way or surgically augmented. Never mind that becoming a dancer, exotic or otherwise, is not among your many aspirations. You're sick of being confronted with the male gaze, telescoped and turned on you, everywhere and every minute. Supermodels and supermoms: sacrifice, modulate your voice, be smart and likable but also fuckable, be the consumable star of an endless soft-porn flick. Thirty-two years you've been on the planet and nothing's new about this, but you may have reached the saturation point with the images flooding your senses. They're depressing enough at the best of times, let alone in your third trimester. And it's a bad time to lose your touchpoints. Your own ideas and standards—of adulthood, of achievement, of beauty—how real are they? How trustworthy? Impending motherhood has crystallized your unease.

The driver doesn't look up when you fail to snatch the transfer she waves in your direction. You make a second grab and get it, forgetting that you don't need it today. It's been your habit to take what is offered. She wears black knit gloves with the fingers cut off. A gold racing stripe divides each fingernail.

"All the way back," she booms, imitating a bullhorn voice.

You decide to resist being treated like livestock. Stand there—no one's getting around your bulk—and look her full in the face.

"Thank you," you say with intense goodwill, spacing each word. "Have a great night."

"Ummm, my night, yep. Move on, little mama."

You flush and consider protesting but reject the idea because you'd look ridiculous, an upholstered woman with a minor grievance. So much for reaching out—was that what you thought you were doing? Better to prepare for the battle ahead.

There are empty seats at the back. You won't have to hang from the ceiling strap, swaying and fuming until someone notices your protruding belly. You could die waiting for that.

Since the pregnancy you've become something of a transit sociologist, mentally filing away the habits of the commuting public. Most people just sit. But sometimes a woman will heave herself out of her seat with a self-satisfied smile. She's been there. She'll feel compelled to disclose how many children she's borne, making your experience, your aches and pains, even your miracle baby, all seem trivial. Countless multitudes of women have survived this; you're no special case. Did you think you were?

Or an old man might stand up, usually so old that you feel it's a legitimate toss-up. He needs to sit more than you do, but will refusing the kind gesture hurt his pride? This sort of social transaction can leave you distracted for hours.

The most likely type to give a pregnant woman his seat is the young man you can think of only as a hood—multiply jewelled, hair-slicked, chewing a toothpick, and probably hopped up on something, but there it is: unfailingly chivalrous. What this says about Toronto early in the twenty-first century you can't begin to guess.

And that's just the seat issue. Don't get started on the folks who can't keep their hands off your middle or say it must be twins—you're so big!—or glare at your coffee. You don't dare snarl back. Your personal belly has become public property. You should get used to it. It's one of the many changes gunning for your so-called normal life.

You make for the back, scoping the car. This crowd looks typical, reading or listening to music in a purposeful way, warding off anyone who might be inclined to chat. They don't have to worry about you.

You notice a man in a grey suit and overcoat with cropped dark hair, third to last row, aisle seat. He wears minimalist glasses in a softer dove grey and reads from an open file folder. The paper on top is stamped "Confidential." A government guy with confidential information. He's the one you're going to sit behind. You might as well learn something while you're stuck between work and home.

You've just hit the seat, have only begun to unclench the muscles supporting your altered centre of gravity, when the singing starts.

Swing low, sweet char-i-ot
Comin' for to carry me home—

You look for the singer out of the corner of your eye. He's standing in the centre of the car, a tall man in a sober dark suit and impeccable white shirt, tieless, slowly turning to stare at each rider in turn, willing a connection. He picked a tough northern place for this kind of thing.

Only two passengers gape openly: a pale girl and boy sitting in side-facing seats toward the front. He has freckles and an innocent, unformed look. His lips are parted, revealing a hunk of pink gum that he's working on and off. She has long, dirty-blonde hair. Her hand is on top of his, pulling his pointer finger down.

They look too young to be riding the streetcar alone, especially in the early dark of winter, but what do you really know about children anyway? How old would be old enough?

Unparented children: they roam the street where your husband has talked you into purchasing a brick semi-detached fixer-upper, its single hallway no wider than the streetcar aisle. A lanky kid showed up the day after you moved in and has been making excuses to chat ever since, stopping by whenever you're in the yard. You like this stray girl well enough and find yourself wanting to take her inside and feed her, an unaccountable desire that's grown over time. But what's the protocol? She swats away queries about parents. Says she's fourteen, but you think maybe eleven. So far, you've resisted inviting her in.

I looked over Jordan, and what did I see-ee?
Comin' for to carry me home?

Your new neighbourhood is a little dodgy, *in transition,* as the real estate agents say, but close enough to the Beaches for them to cash in. The Beaches are getting bigger every day. It's obvious from the westward creep of upscale coffee shops and vintage furniture stores.

Ama-zing grace, how sweet the sound
That saved a wretch like me—

The voice is a deep baritone penetrating your shell. You wonder about *wretch*; wasn't it replaced with something less judgmental? At the moment you feel wretched, a bit nauseous and confined, squeezed into this metal can of malodorous wage-slaves at the end of their day.

You blink back tears. Music often makes you cry. Church music, cancer stories, your boss already discounting every word you say in the run-up to your maternity leave—all of these can open the ducts.

"You need a permit to busk in the transit system," says grey-man from the seat in front of you, looking over the slash of glass hanging low on his nose. He doesn't direct this to anyone in particular.

"I'm glad you asked that, sir." The singer holds the metal pole with one hand, the other on his heart. Sincere.

"I wasn't asking, I was telling." You think of your father and stifle a laugh.

"And I have something to tell *you*. Greatest story ever told." He picks up his worn Bible and waves it in the air. This guy is well put together; you can't help noticing that. He exudes vitality. Unlike anyone else in this streetcar, he loves his job. Which may not even be a job, but a vocation. His mission in life. What would it be like to have one? Maybe you'll find out once the baby arrives. You hope so, because, after nine months of carrying another human being and however many hours of labour will be required to deliver it, not feeling like you had a new mission would be a pretty big problem.

"Let's cut to the chase, folks. You're all bottom-line people," he says. "Who among us has never sinned?" He points around the car. "You? You?" The kids can't take their eyes off him.

You think about this question in spite of yourself. Do you believe in sin? It seems antiquated in a world where all human behaviour can be explained as part of something else, illness or economics or self-preservation. Do you? Don't look at him. Fumble in your bags, finger the cashmere scarf purchased at lunchtime for your husband. Probably your last splurge gift. The financial impact of family responsibility hasn't hit yet. And you doubt your ability to adjust. You were born without the frugality gene.

A girl unfolds her beat-up stroller in the aisle and drops a little boy into it. She reaches up to pull the cord and then angles the stroller forward. Could be the mother or the older sister. She's concentrating. The moment the doors swing open she bumps the stroller down the steps, leading with her baby tilted backwards. You scream and cover your mouth as she pulls back just in time. People around you shift in their seats, putting a few more centimetres of space between you and them. Grey-man lifts his eyes from the page and turns his head to the side, alert, before resuming his reading. What has happened: a car in the curb lane flying past the stop signs. She tries again, not looking upset. The lane is clear this time. For the moment, it's safe to leave the streetcar, exposing her child to whatever may come.

You slump back, thinking: How did I get into this? Even the most careful person, the best mother, can't stop a driver racing the streetcar to the end of the block. Of course, you do realize how you got into this situation. But what are the options, realistically? What is in must come out.

Your dreams have been troubled. You awoke the other night to putting the baby to sleep in the refrigerator, covered in plastic wrap. Not feeling prepared, are you? You're forgetful. How will you remember to put the food in the fridge and the child in the crib?

"What about you, ma'am?" the preacher asks. He noticed

your reaction to the near-accident. He sees everything. "Have you accepted Jesus? Have you invited Him in, opened your door?"

The blood pounds in your ears. Rattle your newspaper so he knows you have other things to do. But something stirs. Maybe it's contempt for the detachment of everyone around, excepting those poor children up front. You want to make amends. You try to answer—what was the question again? Hedge.

"I'm not sure what you mean by that," you say, looking into his eyes at last. They're full of peace, warm and dark in a broad, unlined face. You could hide in those generous eyes.

The preacher continues his patter—you're just a segue for him, which is a kind of relief, to be returned to the ranks of anonymous commuters who happen to be sharing a ride filled with hymns. Yet, he's induced a humming panic in you. What do you believe? How can you be fit to guide a child through life if you don't even know the answer to simple questions?

The streetcar is stopped at River. It should have started moving again by now. The driver's voice cuts to every part of the car.

"You don't got the fare, do you?"

You lean into the aisle to see up front.

"No ride, you got that, Jack?"

A straggled man, too thin, supported by canes, each with a brace where he rests his forearms. He's digging in his pockets. A rustle of impatience rolls through the car—let's go, we're waiting—the sentiment hovers, palpable in the air fogging the windows.

"Know what I'm sick of?" the driver says. "Actors and beggars. Why should I feel sorry for you? I got no time for this show." She shakes her head. "I got the worst route in the system, the worst."

Grey-man closes his file and places it on the seat next to him.

He stands and walks to the front in a no-nonsense way, reaching into his pocket.

"What *you* want?" The driver doesn't turn her head to look at him.

"I'm paying his fare."

"This a charity ride?" She snorts.

"You can't stop me."

"You can pay and pay, but I say who rides. It's my judgment call." She points at the ragged man. "Get off."

He doesn't argue, just turns and struggles down the steps, then crosses in front of the streetcar. You want to shout at him to stay on the sidewalk—don't put yourself in her path, don't be such a pathetic fool. But he makes it to the other side and curves his body into the wind as he starts to shuffle east.

Grey-man shakes his finger in the driver's face. "For shame," he says. You're surprised he would say something like that, charged with old-fashioned moral certainty. "I'm taking your licence down, do you hear me? You're going to lose your job."

She looks in the mirror before releasing the brake. "You want to walk home too, Suit?" She sticks her head out the window and yells at the man on the street. "Ha! Run, cripple! Let me see you run! Ha ha!"

People cluck, but no one else challenges her. It's unsettling to worry about the person piloting the streetcar. Grey-man returns and sits down stiffly. He reaches for his file, holding it closed on his lap. His breathing reaches your ears. You rest your forehead on the seat ahead of you. Your hair brushes his coat.

The preacher sees a new vision of God's work for him. He grabs his Bible and heads for the front, leaving his coat and backpack on the seat. He must be riding all the way out and back tonight, taking his holy-roller show to a captive audience. He crouches behind the driver, whispering. You wonder where his bell and candle are: she's a whack job whose head might start spinning at any moment. The driver starts to laugh, a loud cackle.

Your stop is coming. You gather your things and smile at the children, who, you now realize, belong to your street. Earlier you failed to place them, but they live nearby. Perhaps they'll come visit you, once you're home with the baby. This is the first time a vision of yourself as mother, in a real-life scenario, has come to mind. This thing might actually happen. And you might be okay, transformed into a mother without proper planning. You allow your hand to graze grey-man's shoulder as you pass by, a fluttering pat of appreciation that could be accidental. He doesn't appear to notice.

You haul your belly all the way up front, turning and squeezing. The preacher stands sideways to let you by. Before you can stop yourself, you pull the gift scarf out of the shopping bag and drape it around his neck, reaching up and almost losing your balance as the car jolts to a stop.

"Keep warm." You say this and immediately wish you hadn't spoken. Is the scarf a bribe, an offering to the universe? You're not an everyday hero like grey-man, shoring up humanity with a charitable act. It's safe to say you are confused, careening between anger and peace, optimism and dread. Your intentions are blurred. You want to know the worst outcomes now, before the serious screw-ups, for which you will be blamed, happen.

He touches the scarf, looks at you appraisingly. Wrapping the top of your head with his large hand, he says, "God bless you, sister. And your little one."

"That baby doomed," the driver says. "No-good mother like that, I feel sorry for it."

"Go to hell," you say and lurch down the steps. Immediately you turn and wait for the crowd to disembark so you can go back up and do it right. Your stomach pumps acid as you try to summon better curses, powerful ones to maim the monster who blasted your baby when you weren't yet ready to protect it.

Riders keep coming, bumping your shoulders, annoyed at you for standing so close to the doors. Where are all these people going? They seem to have plans far more elaborate than yours, which, for the next few weeks, is simply survival. Getting through this uncontrollable period with some dignity, if that's possible, and safety, of course. The baby. You have no idea what to do with a baby. Finally, you can't wait anymore.

"Listen, bitch," you scream up at her. "That poor man is dead in the street now, dead at River Street." You look around and open your arms wide to bring the milling crowd onside. Your voice is their call to action, but they're sleepwalkers programmed for home.

"I heard sirens. I saw what you did." You point at her. "Murderer!"

The last person steps down and around you, revealing the driver in the door space, checking her mirrors, lips twitching. She turns to look at you and laughs, shaking her head as the doors shut. The preacher's face appears in a window, his eyes wide and concerned. His lips are moving. The streetcar wheels whine as they begin turning.

"In a hurry? Keeping the schedule? I wait on you for *hours*, lady. Always late." Your voice goes raw. "Fucking bitch, I hope you die in that driver's seat!"

The streetcar pulls away, shuddering, and a freezing wind whips along behind it. You're trembling. Cold and sweaty at the same time. A person who cannot control herself from one moment of human exchange to the next. Someone who should never try to be a mother, that's for sure. You are not the motherly type, although, to be fair, you've never been the deranged screaming type either, until now. You pat yourself down, arranging the bags, and try to slow your breathing. The baby kicks you in the ribs. You deserve that. There are only a few commuters left on the sidewalk. You stand as still as possible and meet the eyes of no one.

Your husband appears out of the night, snow dusting his shoulders.

"Oh good, you're here," he says. "There was an accident. I was afraid you'd be delayed."

"Where?"

"Near the Don River. See it?"

You shake your head, collapse into him, and hand him all your bags. He's not the kind of man to quibble about carrying your purse. You love that about him. He would make a great mom, unlike you.

He talks nonstop during the walk home. He's been working on the house. The nursery is nearly ready to paint. Your role will be picking colours, as you've reached the point of the pregnancy where you should avoid all physical exertion, be gentle with yourself. It's not a good idea to breathe paint fumes or climb ladders, not in your condition. You've been spinning the colour wheel, mulling over the entire spectrum without settling on a shade you can live with long term. You're grateful that your husband will paint the room as many times as you ask him to. You squeeze his arm and think how wonderful it is to make a decision with no consequences. If you choose wrong, just paint over your bad judgment.

Let Heaven Rejoice

Seated at the pipe organ in the overheated choir loft of St. Cecilia's, Mary-Pat Lilly admires her new spring dress draped across her plump but still-good legs. The fabric's repeating lilacs pop against a field of green, jolting her with the energy of Creation's renewal. Her hat, a lavender cloche she's owned for decades, nods cordially to the dress without competing for attention. Remnants of a scent applied to the brim one Easter waft around her head. She inhales faded roses, wondering if the choir has noticed the pleasant smell.

As she extends a foot to the pedal board, the dress slips, exposing her thighs. She tugs the hem down, but it rides up immediately and she leaves it. The choir director won't gawk; he all but ignores her. She smooths the music pages. Her organist's edition of the *Catholic Book of Worship* is worn, its spine split. It will remain open as long as it takes her to play the hymns selected for the tenth Sunday of Ordinary Time.

Her watch reads 10:00 just as the lights in the loft flicker, Father Dan's signal that the altar servers have skidded into line in the vestibule below. Mary-Pat imagines their robes swishing, feels the weight of the crucifix the biggest lad will carry, and the trouble the smaller ones will have balancing tall candles set in heavy gilt bases. She holds her hands above the keyboard and stares down her nemesis, who swivels to face his singers, baton raised. How she relishes this moment before Holy Mass begins: a gathering of grace that will be released when fingers compress keys. The time has come, yet she waits three beats to let the conservatory-educated choir director cool his jets—no, his Jet Ski. She suppresses a giggle. Czernowsky's Jet Ski. She must remember to tell Chevy at dinner—God knows her husband needs a laugh. He's been moping around like a man in over-starched boxer shorts, but she gave up ironing underwear in the '70s. So, she'll tell her instant Polish joke and Chevy will appreciate it. He'll pause over his plate of roast beef, mashed potatoes, and peas, raise his head and say, "Good one, MP." Meaning she's still the one for him after forty-three years, even if certain pistons of the marital engine aren't pumping anymore.

Her hands fall, the processional begins, and parishioners scramble to their feet. She leans into legato notes that vibrate deep in her bones, barely glancing at hymn #557. If she cranes her neck, she can see carved, dark pews lining both sides of the narrow church and a small slice of the light-filled sanctuary. But the organist doesn't have to survey the crowd to visualize the raggedness of their collective rising. She's had a lifetime of Sundays to observe the slovenly and slack-jawed trailing behind the devout who spring to attention and are never clothed in beachwear; the latecomers racing to empty spots before the music ends; the nursing mothers flaunting their bosoms, united in resolute sitting with the so-called invalids of the parish. There's nothing new under the sun, God loves every fallen sparrow, but it's equally true that her church has gone to h-e-double-toothpicks in a ham basket. She gives her all to the music ministry nonetheless; what else can she do?

The second verse ends with a long hold on *Lord*. The choir director's movements become jerky; his apple cheeks redden. Funny, when she first met Martin Czernowsky, his painted-puppet face seemed endearingly childish, a face to pinch rather than smack. Her friends in the Catholic Women's League kept pestering her about the eligible young bachelor who had appeared last fall. How he'd worked miracles with that choir. How he'd make a perfect match for this or that daughter, inevitably a soprano. Rather than confess his aloofness toward her, Mary-Pat let them talk. As if any of their daughters stood a chance with Mr. God's Gift to Music. When angels fly.

Looking for her people among the churchgoers as she plays, she spots the hiked shoulders of her husband in a side pew near the front of the church. He's standing by the aisle next to their daughter, Monica, who probably would have preferred to sit in the back, but Chevy goes up front. Since he got into fitness and lost forty pounds in a month—that unfair way men diet—his navy suit hangs askew. He looks shrunken next to Monica, a big-boned girl. An impulse to reach down and fix Chevy's coat ripples through an octave as she worries the ivory keys.

The procession arrives at the edge of the sanctuary; she has a clear view for an instant before it moves on. First come the readers, one carrying the lectionary. Following them are the altar boys, a snaking line of acolytes stepping not quite to her tempo. She strikes the chords more deliberately, glad to assist the procession on its journey, and is rewarded with a glimpse of her grandson: praying hands, robe too long, innocence incarnate. A shiver of pleasure leaves her jangly in the chest. What a good boy Justin is. He runs to the car when she picks him up every week, not even waving at his lazy parents, who by rights should take him to Mass themselves. She has nearly given up haranguing them, but not quite. Hope springs internal, that's her motto.

Father Dan anchors the procession, as fine a model as any for vocations. Father still visits shut-ins, praises the butter tarts for which the local chapter of the CWL is justly famous, exclaims over newborns and pets alike. So he can't organize his way out of a paper airplane, so what? Most priests need organizers. Mary-Pat has seen them come and go at St. Cecilia's. What sets Father Dan apart is his ability to hew to the middle and avoid parish politics. The grimace he wears today is unusual, though—perhaps a sore tooth. She mentally prescribes her special healing home brew, and if it makes him a little tipsy in the bargain, no harm done. She'll get Chevy to drop it off at the rectory after Mass.

She sings *Raise your voice, be not afraid* and hums the rest of the third verse as she spies her younger son with his new girl-friend on the far side of the church. Sitting by themselves—they probably arrived late and didn't see Chevy. Mark has brought Kara home from the city this weekend to meet the family, but Mary-Pat can't figure out why. Not that she has anything against Asians. On the contrary, she admires their "inane respect for the elderly"—a speaker at last month's regional CWL conference on Aging: Thinking Outside the Box had uttered that phrase and it stuck with her. Inane respect for the elderly—her own kids could use more of that. In Asian cultures, the woman had said, clicking her slides into action, they wouldn't *dream* of incar-cerating their seniors. In fact—a bar graph appeared on the screen—nursing homes don't *exist* in some countries. What's the difference, you may be asking? It all boils down—click-click to the last slide, Aretha Franklin dancing—it's all about R-E-S-P-E-C-T. The CWL ladies had risen as one to applaud.

Goodness, the familiar refrain melts the heart: *let children proclaim to every land.* She ponders the problem of Mark, her only out-of-town child, who rarely visits. Kara being an unbap-tized nothing doesn't faze her; she likes a challenge, and it would be harder to convert a Baptist. No, the problem is Mark's not in love. His posture betrays him: tilted away from Kara, hands in pockets instead of arm around her shoulder. While she's no fan of public displays of groping, she fears there might not be many private ones, either. She wouldn't wish Mark a sexless marriage for all the sake in China.

Her equilibrium falters as a vision overtakes her: lilacs dropping from the sky like St. Thérèse's roses from Heaven, but the lilacs sting her face as though she's being scourged. For what, by Whom, she can't say. And then no lilacs, just black flickering dots. She blinks and swallows the word, "oh." Her throat tightens. Shallow sips of air offer no relief. Perspiration beads under her hatband. What's wrong with her? Woozy, she wills herself to march onward to the final verse. Guide my hands, she prays, and slowly, steadily, builds the wall of sound required to let all creation sing.

Martin Czernowsky's conducting arm begins to ache before they've made it through the processional. Song as battle. Hymns to fight by. Accidents of birth aside, why does he come? Everyone knows the Protestants have better music. His jaw hurts from clenching. Mary-Pat has turned a light piece (saccharine, too accessible, but never mind) into a rafter-shaking dirge. She won't go faster, no matter what he does.

Maybe age dulls the senses. He was almost late this morning because of some geezer stopping for each yellow light. The old guy probably felt like he was racing down the highway. It's like his mother adding more and more sugar to her pies, not perceiving excessive sweetness. She doesn't taste what he tastes, but a dutiful son chokes the pie down. He saw his mother come in earlier and was moved, briefly, by her halting pace as she tapped her cane. She's sitting down there somewhere, the former piano teacher counting six-eight measures and finding fault.

When he raises and lowers his eyebrows in exaggerated time with Mary-Pat's thunder-chords, the choir obliges him by smiling, a difficult feat for mouths rounded into Os. They're good, his choir, especially since Martin recruited the tenors fresh from his old program at the conservatory, twin brothers who so far have delighted him not only with their musicality and taut physical energy, but also their rivalry, openly bidding for Martin's favour. Patience, he thinks, on his optimistic days. Soon. On bad days he's resigned to hapless celibacy.

The choir, his fledglings, would be better served by a skilled accompanist. And a new repertoire: out with the tired ditties and in with complexity. Martin longs to challenge them. Instead, he's a human metronome whipping the air, as the organist—if you can call her that—rocks ponderously, oblivious, crushing beauty.

He turns to study the masses beyond the railing. People are moved, but in the wrong way. Some wear jokey expressions, catching each other's eyes as they vamp the sacred song. Others snap their hymn books shut. They're finished with this dross; if only he weren't associated with it.

He distracts himself from Mass by planning the rest of his day. After a luncheon with his mother that will last too long, he'll discover a headache that prevents him from staying for a watery coffee. Instead, he'll retire to his basement apartment and drown himself in classical recordings for a few hours, headphones insulating his ears as he rests on his futon. Then perhaps he'll see a film or drive into the city in search of an affordable rush ticket to the symphony. He'll go alone, unless he finds the courage to call the tenors. But probably alone.

In the silence that follows the hymn, he takes in Mary-Pat gripping the organ bench, panting. Down below, the first reader steps to the lectern. Father Dan sits in his chair opposite, blank-faced. If he could convince Father to name him music director, he'd find a real organist and shuffle Mary-Pat to Saturday nights. She won't want Saturdays, won't like the nights, especially in winter. He can outwait her, time's on a thirty-year-old's side, but she's taking forever to retire. If she would slide off that bench, the compositions he could tackle.

As a child, he recited nightly prayers with his older brothers and sisters. By the age of six he could produce a flawless Our Father, Hail Mary, Glory Be, and the last, the prayer that wrapped a protective force field around his bed: Angel of God, my Guardian dear, to whom His love commits me here, da-daah, da-daah, da-dum. That was his favourite. His ex-lover, Patrick, thought it odd to have a favourite prayer, but in Martin's family, praying was breathing. Every time the family moved houses, a priest had to sprinkle holy water over their new rooms. Statues of major- and minor-league saints peered calmly from the book shelves. The refrigerator was covered by a disarray of prayer cards pinned with magnets.

He still reveres the prayers for their poetic language, which might as well be tattooed on his body. The words are inescapably his. Nonetheless, his faith in a personal God has long been shaky. If pressed, he'd have to say he worships Art, or maybe God-in-Art, and it's to that faceless entity he appeals with an involuntary spasm as Mary-Pat wallows in the opening notes of the responsorial psalm: please let her just drop dead.

The second reading finds Chevy in the midst of a daydream involving an A-1 babe and a bikini and a beach. It's sunny; there are palm trees and drinks served in hollowed-out pineapples. The gal has an interesting birthmark to show him, right here— whoops, he missed it, he's moving the bathing suit bottom with his work-rough thumb, when she opens her mouth and sings "Proclaim It to the World." With a thud he lands back in church, doomed to relive the opening song. And now they're standing and singing the Alleluia, and it's a tug-of-war. Chevy's not musical—his talent is taking up the collection—but even he notices that people want to go faster. He might not be the smartest guy around, but he understands the agony that settles over the church when someone makes Mass longer than it already is.

Monica nudges his arm and gestures toward the altar boys, where his grandson, Justin, remains seated, staring at nothing, while the other boys all stand at quiet attention. His daughter smiles sympathetically and whispers, "Poor little guy," but Chevy's torn between embarrassment at Justin's error and wanting to rescue him—swooping into the sanctuary, lifting Justin off the pew, onto his shoulders, and outside into the brilliant spring sunshine, a fine escape for both of them. He can almost hear Justin's toddler shrieks of joy. When did the kid become old enough to serve Mass? He feels like he swallowed a rock, the weight of it squashing his chest. Time running. Running out of time. The weight moves lower. He places a hand on his belly, over the bowels that don't move without a blast of dynamite. *Going in for tests, just a few tests,* he rehearses the explanation as sung alleluias rise around him. How he will tell Mary-Pat. How he will avoid telling her until he either has a clean report from the doc or is so obviously riddled with cancer that she figures it out.

The kid should really stand up, though. Justin can be absent-minded—he's a dreamer, more like his uncle Mark was growing up than Justin's own father, Luke. If only—if only a lot of things. Chevy ticks off the rites of passage he should have given his boys but didn't, such as hunting and camping, ice fishing, NASCAR races. Taking them drinking after, shooting the shit. But he was always at work, or else too tired. The adult Mark is a mystery, living far away, changing jobs and girlfriends all the time. And while Luke might be more of a steady-Eddie, working construction to support his wife and kids, lately Chevy strains to find something to talk about with his eldest. It used to be easy. He might still do that guy stuff with Justin someday, with a little planning. But then again, maybe he won't be able to make it happen. And now—he swallows around a swollen throat, snuffles noisily into a handkerchief, and stuffs it back in his pocket— now that bastard Time has him in the crosshairs.

The Alleluia is almost over, the Gospel about to begin. He stares hard at Justin, willing him to rise. Don't they train altar boys anymore? He still remembers the drill from his youth, the whole shebang. Everything in Latin back then. Those memories are fresher than yesterday: the freezing church, his balls shrivelled beneath threadbare, patched pants, his knees knocking. Trudging to church on dark, snowy mornings, his inadequate leather boots. And sour arthritic Monsignor Cleary—in his grave these many years, the old drunk—who would rap the boys' knuckles afterward without explaining what it was they had done or failed to do. Chevy bet he could still perform the altar boy's duties if he were suddenly pressed into service: to stand, kneel, ring the bells, scurry to hand the priest the right objects in the right order at the right time; to remain poker-faced and hide the yawns. At the front of the church, the tall robed boy next to Justin looks down and, without changing expression, subtly tugs Justin's sleeve, pulling him to his feet. Chevy relaxes. He barely has time to form an approving thought about the older lad, surely a priest in the making, when Justin opens his mouth wide for a long toothy yawn. He flinches, while Monica buries her snort of laughter in his shoulder.

The singing stops but the organ continues as Mary-Pat takes a victory lap around the Alleluia and Father Dan waits, his mouth a thin line.

God, it's awful.

He covers his face with his hands, feeling the stubble he

missed while shaving. He's sorry for Mary-Pat, he really is, despite the fact that she won't stop watching him now that he's given up drinking and started walking in the evenings. She keeps asking where he's walking to. Why does it have to be anywhere? he answers. Once she said, "Hmmph. Mid-life crisis," and he barked that she must be pretty daft if she thinks seventy-three is mid-life. She's a hound sniffing for clues. Plainly, she suspects a gal on the side. Well, not anymore, lady. If only he could have those days back.

What will happen to all of them? *Just a few tests. Don't borrow trouble.* But he can't help fearing the ordeal ahead, the burden on his family. His decline, and after. How will they remember him, when he's gone? *Wait for the tests.*

Christ, Mary-Pat and her attack on the instrument. She practises faithfully on the tinny electric organ at home but never improves. How will she fill her time when she can't play anymore? For years since his retirement, her practice schedule has allowed him to disappear for an afternoon without attracting attention. He'd slip away to secret pals and secret dives, joints she'd never been to, which might have been the most attractive thing about them. And now he's quit the drinking in a leap of faith. He should have listened to the health nuts earlier, reformed his bad ways.

He presses his fingers into bloodshot eyes, sparking flashes. It's too late to pry the box of his choices open, even if he wanted to. It's all too complicated to sort out. Sweet Jesus, let something be over. He's tired. Let it end soon, one way or another.

Father Dan peers over his reading glasses at the two boys flanking the lectern, each hugging a candle half their height, shifting foot to foot. He shuffles papers, adjusts the mic. Scripture can't be altered, of course, but he'll keep the homily short to make amends for what they have to listen to. He does recognize an upside to the music: people pray harder while they're here. That's a plus.

He intones, "The Gospel according to St. Luke," making the sign of the cross on his forehead, lips, and breastbone, and the congregation mirrors his movements, an amplification that nourishes him. Faith manifested bodily: statement, symbol, and action, simultaneously internal and external—he lives for this. Immediately afterward, though, reading Luke's account of Jesus raising a widow's son from the dead, his thoughts drift. A few ladies approached him yesterday, members of the CWL at war. He sighs, wishing he hadn't seen the letter that appeared in his mailbox afterward, a missive one faction plans to send in support of some radical nuns on a bus trying to break into the priesthood. Nuns on a bus. A mental image of wimpled, wizened faces peering crossly from the windows of a yellow school bus tickles his lips. Not that kind of nun, he reminds himself, sobering. He pictures guitar-strumming sisters in A-line skirts and low-heeled sandals, outwardly meek yet willing to chain themselves to the gates of nuclear facilities and challenge Holy Mother Church at every turn. Someone photocopied the letter and sent it to him anonymously, hoping he'd intervene against the looming danger of women priests. Some days the CWL torments him. Don't they realize he'd rather chat and charm? He makes ceremonies of receiving their bake-sale proceeds, isn't that enough?

"Place yourself in the widow's shoes," he says. "Feel her desperation turn to jubilation when the miracle is performed." His speech quickens, perhaps to outpace the bickering females in his head. Is he supposed to report the letter-writers to the bishop? Advise them not to send the letter despite his personal views? Join them and *sign* the letter? He finds himself strangely indifferent to the scandal that would cause.

Extemporizing, he draws parallels to modern medicine, seemingly miraculous, and yet nothing can touch the scene in Judea, which hinges on a woman's simple belief. He envisions disbanding the CWL, locking all the ladies out of the parish kitchen, stamping his foot, sidestepping. His view is framed by candles held aloft. The light wavers, dancing and bending. He softens, takes a breath, and tries to wrap up.

He's mid-sentence when the smallest altar boy darts across to assist one of the candle-bearers struggling to rebalance his load. The taper tilts. The boy reaches for it as it falls, catching the billowy curtain enveloping his arm. It happens so fast that Father can't do a single useful thing in response to the gasps of people in the front pews. What is that child's name—Jordan, Jayden?—no, Justin. The organist's grandson, God love him.

A spark, a flaring at the edge of the boy's sleeve. His face twitches: horror. He tries to run, but two men spring forward to catch him in the centre aisle, and Father knows without having to look that one of them is Chevy. Wordlessly, they tackle the boy and roll him between them. The younger man—doesn't he know him? One of Chevy's boys?—lies prostrate in the aisle, covering Justin with his body. Like a supplicant, like a priest being ordained. Father darts from behind the lectern. He belongs with them, his people in need. As he reaches the trio, the man rolls off the boy and pulls him into an embrace while Chevy crouches nearby, awkwardly patting his grandson. He's fine, thank heaven. No worse for the wear.

Music swells: the offertory hymn too early, *lentamente* and *fortissimo*. Laughter, then applause, erupts. Father shakes Chevy's hand and says, "This is your part, my friend."

Justin returns to the altar servers, solemn and pale, and Chevy's son—Mike? Mick?—to his attractive companion. Chevy trolls the aisle, passing the collection basket.

Seated, Father closes his eyes. He doesn't have anything to do with the candles. The head server prepares the altar before every Mass, gliding importantly across the carpet in sock feet, silent except for the click of the barbecue lighter—they haven't struck matches in ages. After Mass, a younger boy is deputized to blow the candles out. It's no one's fault, but he'll have to call a meeting to review procedures. A small hassle—gratitude anoints him, leaving no room for irritation. How much worse the accident could have been. He draws his fingers to his lips, pondering the nature of miracles, and floats a petition to the Lord: might an inconvenient letter be destroyed through some joyful, as yet undiscovered, mystery?

The offertory hymn claims Mark's racing pulse, insisting on a slower pace, but he resists. Kara puts her arms around his waist and squeezes. She says something in his ear that his mother's relentless playing blocks. She tries again. "God saved him. God saved him through *you*." He peels her off and nods at the altar, where the Eucharistic rite is in progress. She drops to her knees, a thing he's never seen her do in a church. Which leads—he can't help it—to a looping clip of the two of them naked, blurry and out of context. She falls, she goes down; he banishes each image as the next arrives. They roll around his mind, but he feels no desire for her, which is strange. Lust has kept him with Kara for six months. It's been the constant of their relationship. But now—he looks at her breasts, remembers last night—no, nothing. He can't catch his breath; it's as though he was sprinting uphill on his bike. He tries to calm himself by remembering how his second wind kicks in just when he thinks he'll collapse from exhaustion; how the rhythm of pedalling takes over.

When it's time for the congregation to kneel together, he remains standing. Steady, he tells himself, but he can't think over the pounding in his ears. The fuck, what the fuck, what the—?

He sees the priest notice them out of sync and pretend not to notice. Folding his arms, he feels not his own torso, but the imprint of his nephew. Brave boy. No crying, jumped back in line with the big kids, but the tremors passed through him as he pinned Justin to the floor. The smell of singed cloth lingers. His legs fail, and then he, too, kneels. Kara weeps silently, dripping on the pew in front of them. He doesn't comfort her. If he were to smash every gilded, glittery object, where would he start? The candle stands.

At Communion, Kara gets in line, although his mother told her not to. "I'm afraid you, as a non-Catholic, dear, are ineligible to receive the Host," she had said, patting Kara's hand. "Don't take it personally." The music starts: "Be Not Afraid," #481, played in the contemplative style of a dying animal. He stays behind. When Kara reaches the front, she falls at the priest's feet, arms crossed over chest; her shoulder blades heave as she receives his blessing. Mark slumps, head on hands: no, no, no. He half expects Kara to crawl back to her seat, a penitent pilgrim, but Father gently pulls her up, and she walks like a normal person who hasn't been touched by divine intervention. In an instant, the things that had been so good between them flipped to intolerable. He can't say why, but neither can he deny it. They are finished.

She slides in; he shifts away. He's not interested in her revelation. He's not her witness. They were going to stay another night and return to the city tomorrow, but that's impossible. He just has to get through one more meal at home—the avid questions from his mother and sister as they appraise Kara; the vague disapproval beneath his father's grunts and nods—and then the relationship will collapse.

He fortifies himself against the crashing music, against stale ritual and predictable commentary in the vestibule after Mass is over. It *is* over, for him. Why has he been going to church all these years? Inertia. And what a mistake it was, dragging Kara here. From now on, he'll spend Sunday mornings like the rest of the world: sleeping in, making love, biking with friends, whatever freedom offers: he is free.

Up in the choir loft, Mary-Pat hangs on. She can make it to 11:00, God willing. She frowns, thinking of the congregation applauding a few minutes ago. That wasn't right. It's nice to be appreciated, but clapping is too much. She doesn't go in for dog-and-phony shows.

She turns at last to the recessional hymn: sprightly, yes, *let's*. But the notes stick to her fingers like leeches in a muddy river, and she's pulled beneath the surface. Panic fills her, then numbness. She scarcely feels the keys carving indentations in her cheek; or sees stricken Martin working his cell phone to summon help; or hears the discordant notes that wail without end from her instrument. She rests, semi-conscious, on the keyboard.

A white light blinds her—not the peaceful light of acceptance she's read about, more like driving through dense fog on a winding road as cars whip around to pass her. She darn well likes to see where she's going. But just in time a gift of grace arrives. She grasps the brilliance of God's plan: a painless, happy death, what everyone hopes for, and here at the organ, how fitting. She doesn't mind that her hat is crushed and her dress sweat-soaked. She doesn't worry about the next song. She dribbles spit on the keys and feels no shame for what she's powerless to change. Martin hovers nearby, saying her name, prompting an uncharitable thought—*he* won't be sorry—before she remembers the need to keep her soul stainless at this critical stage. She's done her best—hasn't she? All she can do is ask to be forgiven.

She has no idea how much time passes before she regains the

powers of movement and music. As she lifts her head from the keyboard and the smashed notes die, just one truth rings clear: she's still here.

If Mary-Pat had been promoted to angel, she wouldn't need a flyover to know what's happening at St. Cecilia's this morning. She'd feel the Mass suspended on a sound that calls to mind an oncoming freight train, everyone gaping at the choir loft except Father Dan, who stands, head bowed, straining to hear a message in the din. She'd understand why Chevy bolts through the side door onto the street while Mark pounds up the stairs to reach her, and Kara distracts Justin by leading him to the statue of St. Thérèse of Lisieux, where they kneel together and read about the Little Flower's life. Mary-Pat, more than anyone, would enjoy seeing Justin push Kara's change into the coin box, choose an extra-large votive candle, and light it, but, not being an angel yet, she can't.

At the Track

The summer of 1975, my grandfather's friends wore leisure suits in turquoise and moss and mulberry with patterned shirts left open a few buttons to reveal an overgrowth of chest hair, but Grandpa refused to update his tailored black suits and cufflinked shirts. One night, the night I was taken to Monticello Raceway for the first time, Grandma challenged the men.

Why you wanna upstage the ladies? She patted her platinum up-do. I'm the colourful one. They raised a glass to her glory, and she struck a pose: shoulder forward, eyebrow raised, hand on throat, a movie star you could name if you thought about it long enough.

We watched the races on a monitor in the track lounge, a smoky room filled with patrons seated at round tables. As the horses entered the home stretch, Grandma touched her golden pin, a miniature jade-eyed racehorse and driver with filigree whip unfurled. Everyone leaned forward and then fell back into their chairs, except for Bean. He hooted, opening and closing his legs in triumph.

Aww, it's still early, Grandpa said, tearing his ticket in half.

Bean crossed the hallway to the cashier's window to claim his prize and then returned to us. Bald and squat, he moved like the wrestler he once was: power under pressure.

Between races, Bean and the other guys entertained me. Now you see kids everywhere—Atlantic City, Vegas—but back then I was the only one initiated into rituals of chance that drew my grandparents three or four times a week. I knew it was special.

The fact that my mother had no idea where I was only sweetened the pot. This was around the time my parents split up. My father had cashed in his chips, Grandpa said once, when he thought I wasn't listening. Dad moved out of state and stayed gone. Mom had just started nursing at the hospital, taking every night shift she could get, so she relied on her parents, much as she hated to do it. From a young age, she'd felt an unnatural burden of responsibility. To hear her tell it, she was the only grown-up, the one who kept order in the house and looked after her younger siblings, while her parents went to clubs and partied until dawn. To her, they were like highly emotional children in need of regulation. Once, scrubbing our countertop furiously, she said, The crumbs in that house. Mouse droppings in the silverware drawer. Junk everywhere. You have no idea, Ann. It felt like an argument, even though I stayed silent. I was the prize in their long-running battle. I was the pawn.

She'd object, with a tight shake of her head, when Grandpa gave me sips from his wineglass at Sunday dinners filled with cousins and aunts and uncles, all shouting happily that there was no harm in it. It made her miserable to be overruled, when, by maternal rights, she should have had the final say over what I ingested. No one believed Grandma when she promised to enforce early bedtimes for me, those nights my mother worked, and to feed me sensible food and no junk. She'd say anything to keep me away from sitters who weren't blood relations. Even though their people had been in America for three generations, my grandparents still held old-country values. Paying strangers to babysit wasn't one of them.

My mother didn't get the concept of playing with money. It's a big con, she often said, referring to the horses, but also the lottery tickets and the card games, all their entertainments. She was the only one of their children to get an education beyond high school and, Grandma once said, darkly, the only one ashamed of where they came from. It might have been education that separated Mom from the family, but I think it was genetics. She was the odd introvert born to a mob of huggers and kissers. There wasn't a thing she inherited from them except her looks: the dark eyes, long lashes, and curly black hair, exactly like Grandma's before she went platinum blonde.

After work, Mom sat with her feet in a bucket of water, tapping her cigarette on the tiled metal ashtray that I made at school for Mother's Day by cementing one green square after another in wobbly circles. Don't be fooled, Ann, she told me. They lose as much as they win—more. I wish they'd stop running around with those seedy friends.

But I liked them: Bean and Rat, with his pockmarked face and whispery voice; Roy and Johnny, brothers who went home for their mother's baked ziti at lunchtime; and Sam, a lawyer who'd been *disbarred*, which I thought meant let out of jail.

They blew smoke rings in a competition, releasing skyward exhalations. Every attempt was followed by an uproar from the table, full of insults and arm-slapping. When Grandpa puffed out a perfect halo, Roy elbowed Bean. Who died? he said. Guy dresses like that, he's in mourning. Or an undertaker.

Grandpa stirred his whiskey with his pinkie. He snorted. Peacocks! You look like goddamn peacocks in them swishy getups.

Vincent, Grandma said. God is listening to every word you say. She turned to me. Do you want another Shirley Temple, Anna? Have another, why not?

I slurped the last of my drink, smiling around the straw. No one else called me Anna. This was another way she claimed me, recasting my anglicized given name to draw it closer to hers. Shirley Temple was my favourite: pink fizz, parasol, maraschino. Also, of course, the child star of my grandmother's youth, her fantasy Hollywood best friend. Grandma prayed for Shirley to be cured of her recent illness—*breast cancer*, always stage-whispered—and the inner turmoil that caused it. I can still see her performing "On the Good Ship Lollipop," mimicking Shirley's babyish singing, shuffling through the dance steps, surprisingly light on her feet. Afterward, she curtsied and blew kisses as the men applauded. Brava, Annamaria! Brava!

She called the waitress, who came running, wiping her hands on her apron. Ginny will take care of us, she said, and it was true. Ginny knew without being told that we wanted the shrimp scampi, rare steak, and onion rings.

Dessert win or lose, right? Ginny asked. As she leaned over to collect the empty glasses, Grandpa pinched her rear, causing her to jump. Everyone laughed—even she couldn't keep a straight face, scolding him. And nothing for you, mister!

Then it was finger tricks. Watch this, Rat said, sliding his hands together and apart, together, apart, severing his index finger at the first knuckle. Rat had yellow-stained fingertips and nails like claws, which seemed ominously connected to the pale scooped-out spots on his face. A cupping sound came from his hands as they made contact. Isn't that something? Betcha can't do that with *your* finger, girlie.

I fished the maraschino cherry out of my glass and handed it to him. Show me how to tie the stem with your tongue, I said. Grandpa always did that, tight-lipped while he swallowed the cherry, worked the stem, and finally stuck his tongue out, revealing the knotted filament. Whenever I asked Grandpa to teach me, he said, Nah, that'll spoil it.

Rat looked uncomfortable as the others yelled, Oh, the cherry, oh oh!

He gave it back to me. Geez, don't think I know that one.

Bean chortled. Word on the street is he don't know what to do with that tongue of his. It's kinda retarded. Anyway, that's what the ladies say. Johnny pounded the table; Grandpa gasped for breath. But Grandma frowned, and Bean straightened up. Forget that old chestnut, he said. What's this? He tapped his heels on the floor in rhythm.

Bean's zip-up boots rose and fell. I was mesmerized by the vulnerable strip of white, hairless skin just below his pant leg, and at the same time, I wished he would cover it. He slapped his thighs, following the same giddy-up beat. Horses, I said. Hoof-beats. I rolled my eyes.

Smart cookie there, Bean told Grandma, reaching for my cheek. I saw his pudgy hand and gold rings coming at me but didn't shy away from the pinch. He passed a five-dollar bill across the table. Trust luck, he said. It's in your blood.

Sam clinked my drink with his. He's right. Good luck skips a generation.

I folded the money into the palm of my hand and looked at Grandma. She nodded. Go ahead, give it a whirl.

First, I climbed to the observation deck. High in the open-air stands, I studied the horses warming up—magnificent beasts charging the track until the jockeys pulled them into a walk and turned back for another lap. The precarious grace of those drivers: shirts bright as flags, perched atop careening carts with flashing, clacking wheels. Trotter, jockey, sulky, silks, I chanted. A black horse barrelled past me, nostrils flared. Number ten, and I was ten that summer. My first bet.

Grandpa never looked at the horses. His system was doodled on the racing form: sires and dams, odds and owners, underlines and check marks. Grandma's approach was to play her numbers—1, 3, 4—and pray. The Lord's been good to me all these years, she'd declare, as the men continued stories of deals gone sour, cataloguing the slights, grudges, and feuds in their circle. Time after time, her numbers proved more powerful than Grandpa's pen. How he loved her.

The tired clerk sat behind brass bars, slumped on her elbow, reading a movie magazine. She didn't look up as I approached on tiptoe, until I pushed the five bucks toward her. Her eyes widened. I must have been a sight: a homely, underage customer in a Fonzie t-shirt and pigtails. When I said number ten Joyride, she just smirked and gave me the ticket. She didn't need to hear my ready lies.

The bells chimed a warning. The race was about to start. I dropped my ticket on the table. Well! What's your pick? Grandma scanned my face seriously, as if considering whether or not I had her gift. I told her, and she nodded, satisfied. Here we go, she sang, fanning herself with tickets.

The announcer called names—my horse somewhere in the middle of the pack. The air was close and hazy, the TV too remote. I wanted to see the race myself. There wasn't much time—I ran as fast as I could through the stands and stood at the rail, letting the night breeze cool my face, cheering. Hoofbeats thundered. I began jumping up and down. My horse was in the lead as they rounded the final turn, but right away two others came up the inside, and the announcer started yelling. Flashbulbs popped, everyone screamed, and I stood very still.

IIIIT'S NIIIIGHTSHADE by a nose, the announcer boomed. NIIIGHTSHADE. KIIING OF ARABIA. JOOOY-RII-IDE. I gasped, not realizing that I'd been holding my breath until the end. Still not believing that number ten, my own Joyride, could be a loser, I crumpled my ticket.

At our table, everyone was hugging each other except Grandpa, who was concentrating as he checked and rechecked Grandma's ticket. I'll be damned.

My grandmother landed a loud smooch on his cheek. The fur coat, Vince! You have to say yes now. I'm picking it out tomorrow.

He opened his hands. How can I argue with this beautiful woman? Why not? Easy come, easy go.

I nuzzled Grandma's side. She put her arm around me and took my ticket in one smooth motion. Let's see ... you won, too!

I shook my head. I lost.

You bet to Show. Win-Place-Show, see? You're in the money, honey. Go get your winnings.

I returned to the lady in her cage and slid my wrinkled ticket under the bars. She beamed, counting out twelve dollars. Beginner's luck! Come back soon, dear. And I did return, too many times to count. After that first night, I was never again afraid to approach a betting window.

Back at the table, I touched the cash in my pocket. Later, I'd buy myself a rabbit's foot and earrings for my mother, who worked hard and deserved a nice surprise. Her face was puzzled as I gave her the box. She asked and asked, dimming the shine of my gift, but I never admitted where the money came from.

The hoopla went on for some time. Grandma's numbers beat long odds for the Trifecta, with the payoff more than fifteen thousand, a number I couldn't comprehend.

The Lord has been so very good—

Drink, Annamaria! Drink to victory.

Round's on us, Grandpa said, signalling Ginny. He slipped a hundred-dollar bill into the front of her blouse, and she let him.

Then he gave Rat the winning ticket, holding Rat's hand for a moment inside both of his big hands. Find Billy.

Who's Billy? I asked.

Just a guy we know, Grandpa said. He handed me a frosty glass with a striped parasol floating on top.

A gimp-leg bum, Grandma said. He'll cash it for us.

Only chumps tell the taxman. Grandpa pointed at me. Remember that.

Amen, Bean said. Never tell 'em a thing.

Rat soon returned with Billy, a grizzled coat hanger of a man wearing baggy trousers, with one normal shoe and the other built on a thick platform sole. His hands were in his pockets as he limped toward us.

Billy laid three bricks on the table—fifties wrapped with paper bands. Grandma gave one to Grandpa, who broke it open, peeled off some bills, and handed them to Billy. Thanks, he said. Pleasure doing business again. Billy waited for a second longer, ducking his head at Grandma, and then me, before leaving. Grandpa gave more bills to Rat, who nodded, pushed them into his pocket, and walked away.

Grandma stuffed the other bricks into her bosom mountain, one on each side. You'd never know unless you saw it go in—the little gold horse glittered just the same, trotting across the same rise and run of her blouse, but now worth a lot more. *The boobie bank*, my mother liked to call it, in contrast with the real bank where she *securely* deposited her funds. Grandma gave more cash to Ginny, who squealed and embraced her. I showed everyone my twelve bucks. Like attracts like, Grandma said, throwing a fifty at me.

We were dipping into the cherry cobbler when Rat came up. Gotta go, he said in his soft rasp. Now. We looked at him, spoons in mid-air.

What's up? Johnny said. He and Roy exchanged glances.

Rat licked his lips. Braganzolo.

Swankie Frankie Braganzolo, Johnny said, and rose to his feet. Must want to collect from you, Vince, now you're flush. Wants his loan paid ahead of schedule. Just like that bastard. Sam and Bean nodded. Sam put his sunglasses on.

Grandpa dropped cash on the table, and Grandma was already tying her chiffon scarf around her neck as she slung her purse over her arm and pulled me up.

Goddamn bum can't keep his mouth shut, Grandpa said. That's the last time we use him.

What about dessert?

Another time, dear.

Who's Swankie Frankie?

Just a guy we know, Grandma said.

Why does he want to get paid?

Doesn't everyone? Let's go, honeybunch.

Grandma and Grandpa pulled me between them. I turned around and saw the men fanning out behind us, pretend-casual. Bean winked, but he didn't crack a smile.

We shouldn't have brought her, Vince. Grandma's voice shook. Now what have we done?

No time for yakking, Grandpa said. Hustle. Do the hustle! He playfully lifted me into the air and then set me down again as we race-walked. I clutched their hands and took three steps for each of theirs.

Grandma huffed. What are we going to tell her mother?

Jesus, not now. Grandpa's face was red. He wasn't used to hustling.

As we got closer to the car, I started running, like in the movies when the good guys are making a break for it. I threw myself against the shiny black Cadillac, hugging cool metal. Grandpa and Grandma were right behind me, both breathing hard. Grandpa turned out of the parking lot, and the tires squealed.

The back seat of the Caddy was big and deep, perfect for a girl who liked to bounce. There were no rules in the back seat. When I got tired of up and down, I slammed from one door to the other as Grandpa took the curves fast. He lit a cigarette and rolled down the window, checking his rear-view mirror. The wind whipped my hair, the best feeling of all. It meant summer, the expansiveness of nights with my grandparents before they had to surrender me back to my mother. The knots in my hair would go untended until I returned home in the morning, when I would have to submit to my mother's combing them out. Riding fast and free was stolen time.

Grandma dabbed at her temples with an embroidered handkerchief, and I caught her scent of spicy cologne.

You're sweating, I said.

She looked at Grandpa, who smiled at me in the mirror, and then she twisted around to face me. Horses sweat, men perspire, and ladies glow. Remember that. She reached out and pinched my cheek, much gentler than Bean. Turning back to Grandpa, she rested her hand on the back of his neck, just above the starched white collar.

Can you believe that goddamn bum.

Please, Vincent. Leave God out of it. They were silent for a long time. I stopped bouncing and laid my cheek on the cool, embracing leather, watching the road signs whip past. We sped along the highway through dark tunnels of trees.

There they are, Grandpa said. Two cars came from behind, lighting the road ahead of us, honking their horns. Grandpa honked back as they passed. That's our convoy. You get a fur coat, guess what I'm getting? One of them CB radios like the truckers.

Truckers! Look at the fine fabric on this suit. Grandma stroked his lapel. Hey, what do you say we stop for pizza? I bet our girl back there is hungry.

If we had a CB, you could call the boys and ask do they want pizza.

We stopping or not?

Ten-four, big mama.

Big! She punched his shoulder lightly.

Grandpa roared ahead and swung around the other cars, drag racing. I let out a whoop, and he grinned. "It's JOOOYRII-IDE by a NOOOOSE," I shouted, and Grandma cheered me on, clapping. I don't remember them ever shushing me. He pulled the Caddy off the road, heading for a joint with pulsing neon lights, and the guys followed.

Midnight pizza, pizza for winners, ha! Grandma faced me again, serious now. Don't go telling will you, Anna? Tonight's our little secret. She pulled me half into the front seat for a squeeze. My bella! You're going to be a model when you grow up, bet on it.

Well, that was never in the cards. I wanted to inherit her glamour and beauty, but what I got was her luck.

Five or six years later, she and Grandpa moved in with us, and not by choice. They lost the Cadillac, so no more Monticello, and off-track betting hadn't been invented yet—they would have loved OTB as much as I do. My mother gave them an allowance of twenty-five dollars a week for lottery tickets: a laughable amount, pitiful to them, yet it killed her to part with the cash, knowing they'd blow it. I guess it was her way of showing love; I'm able to see that now. I remember sitting with them at night, doing my homework, chewing a pencil over math problems as they scraped the tickets with quarters, looking for a jackpot or a few bucks, anything worth celebrating. We'd make a pile of crumbs from the silver seals on their tickets and the red remains of my eraser, pushing them across the tabletop, and at the end we'd whisk them onto the carpet, ta-dah! My mother would be upstairs alone, vacuuming, or banging pots against our cozy conspiracy.

I knew their high spirits were an act for me. Cut off from their friends, stuck in our basement, they had nowhere to go. Grandpa's emphysema tethered him to an oxygen tank. He gave up careful dressing, wearing the garish golf shirts my mother bought on sale in packs of three. One man, seven days in every week, how many shirts did he need? He didn't even perspire anymore. But she kept buying them. She wanted to be a good daughter, and I guess she was. Seeing him in clown orange and happy-face yellow was beyond depressing. He's not a goddamn peacock, I yelled once, but Mom ignored my outburst.

Hey, I don't like to dwell on their long decline. They were a show worth watching, a hell of a joyride—give them that. I'm glad they're riding wild across the sky, all losses forgotten. And now that I'm my own mother, my own grandmother, what I remember is winners racing darkness home; Caddy backseat bouncing perfectas; horses straining for the finish line, jockeys whipping them on; and the payouts, the smell of bills large and small. The thrill of the first bet never fades. Scribbling the odds, stroking the jade-eyed golden horse that is now pinned to my blouse, I'm at the track more often than not, watching my picks, hoping for a payday. Here's to the race, I say, and to the people who brought me here. Here's to joyriding, free of sleep.

The Winnings

Where's the big man got to?" my mother said, running a finger under her watchband to scratch her puffy wrist as she checked her watch. "Six-thirty. He should've been here an hour ago."

"Do you want to go to dinner?" I said. She hated to eat late. There'd be another wait at the restaurant. But she settled her bulk into my living room easy chair, deciding for us. She had come straight from the salon, and I was still getting used to her new hairdo, a series of twirls and fillips piled into a high fortress glued with smelly product, and the dramatic jet black she had chosen. My hair was naturally auburn, and hers had always been dark brown, lately greying. Until now. Black hair made her skin seem paler than ever, and for the first time, I noticed white patches of scalp showing through at the temples.

"We can't celebrate without Kyle. He's a good man, Allison. Treat him like a king and you'll have no regrets."

"But you're hungry," I said. "You must be, hallucinating about marriage like that. When did you ever treat Dad like a king?"

"Don't be a brat. I can wait to eat. We should wait for Kyle." She smoothed her aqua stretch pants along the thighs and then folded her arms across her floral print sweater set. A crumpled Kleenex was jammed into one sleeve.

I began smoothing the ripped thighs of my jeans, until I realized I was imitating her, so I got up to stretch. I needed to move, to be doing something besides waiting. "Suit yourself. Who knows—maybe there was a mix-up with the ticket."

I stood at the window and watched cars idling at the stoplight, the last trace of rush hour, as she wheezed behind me. Staring at traffic gave me a vision of Kyle, car windows down all the way, music thumping, driving in the wrong direction. Speeding away from home, and me, the jackpot money chasing him down the highway. It came to me so clearly. I knew he'd chosen the off-ramp.

"It's probably construction. He'll be here," she said, as if her saying so would make it happen. Once she'd decided something, she wouldn't admit to being wrong, even if she later changed her mind and shifted direction. She'd just barrel on at the same speed as before, not pausing to reflect.

"Have it your way," I said, snapping the curtains closed, and then, remembering that I needed to keep watch, opened them again.

Her sudden faith in Kyle was hard to take. Until he hit his numbers two weeks ago, she kept hinting that he was a poor bet.

"The father took off, do I have that right?" she said in July, placing her icy drink against the back of her neck for a moment before slurping it. "That kind of thing repeats in families. It's a cycle, you better believe it." I didn't answer. And neither did I believe that Kyle would abandon me, as his father had done when Kyle was a baby. His mother destroyed all the photos; he had no memory of a father but didn't seem troubled by that history.

And in August when I should have been going away to

school but didn't, she said, about Kyle but, really, about both of us, "Factory work's no future. Where's his get up and go?"

I guess he found it on the 401 Highway. The oversized white-board cheque must have been propped against the passenger seat, five zeros daring him to make the big U-turn.

Kyle worked shifts at the cardboard plant. He had considered higher education on and off, but the steady money was too good to give up. Five years out of high school, he was still there. As for myself, I couldn't seem to decide on a next step, moving from one low-paying job to the next. I was cleaning cottages, but that gig would end once winter came.

"Can't see taking the chance on university now, with the recession," he'd said to me as we walked the streets one evening, holding hands, following the riverside trail.

"Let's not," I answered, syncing our steps. We grew up in this small city on the edge of the big city. "Look at all this," I said, with a sweep of my hand, taking in the houses and trees, the river rolling past. "It's everything. How could we leave it?"

"The world will always need boxes," he said. "That's all I know."

While Mother dreamed up problems stemming from our failure to go on with our schooling—"A privilege I never had," she reminded us repeatedly—I planned the wedding: not too big, not too small, the white dress, traditional.

If Kyle had come back, it would have been next weekend. The weather channel promised a cool but sunny day, the fall foliage at peak viewing pleasure for tourists and locals alike. Scattered fall leaves, orange and yellow and red, were printed on our invitations and napkins and matchbook covers along with our intertwined initials, the reception swag thematically aligned. There would be pots of cheap and cheerful mums on every table, in case anyone missed the fact that it was fall, the season of crisp new chances.

And now she had turned into the wedding cheerleader. She couldn't stop bragging about her future son-in-law. Hadn't she herself cleaned up in the bingo halls? They had good luck in common. Kyle and Allison were meant for each other. They had a bright future ahead, the best.

She heaved herself up and headed for the kitchen, saying, "Isn't there anything to drink in this place?"

I nodded wearily, but she was already gone. She knew where to find the booze. I heard clinking bottles, and she came back with a tray: scotch for herself and red wine for me.

"You should get a treatment before the wedding," she said. "No charge."

I took the wineglass and peered through it, rolling the glass across the bridge of my nose, drowning my eyes in the wavy maroon vista.

"I don't think so." I was calm. Resolved, not sad. The idea of that needle jabbing my skin reminded me of porcupine quills in my late dog's muzzle, the suffering he had to endure before the vet put him under. And besides, the wedding was off.

"This is no time to give up on grooming. You want to look good walking down that aisle." She patted her updo, needlessly. It was still solid, not a hair mussed.

"I'm not worried." She wanted me to worry, that was the point. To waste time fretting about things that didn't matter. I sipped my drink and thought of her working on clients, day after day. She didn't see the person on her table, only a map of pores and hairs magnified beyond all decency as she burned each follicle with electric pulses. I'd spent summers as her receptionist; I knew how she was, torturing clients in the name of beauty.

"Stubborn like your father." She'd be onto him next, expecting me to agree. He had a body shop in an adjoining garage that smelled of Varsol. People brought their fender benders out back to him, and some of them went to her for electrolysis, even men.

Poor Dad, he still blushed at any mention of the aesthetic operation on the street side of his business, as if he could pretend it wasn't there. He probably would have liked being father of the bride, even while he braved the attention that came with walking me down the aisle. The father–daughter dance a nightmare for him, but he'd have done it. I would have to break the wedding news to him myself. Not Mother. She'd twist the explanation into an episode in which he was somehow at fault for chasing Kyle away. But he liked Kyle well enough, didn't he? I realized that Dad had not expressed an opinion on the subject. At least, not to me.

"And what's wrong with a clean jaw line on the most important day of your life?" Her pencilled eyebrows rose above her sparkly glasses in two accusing brown arcs. I wanted to point out that she should change her pencil to black to match her new hair, but I swallowed that thought with a gulp of wine.

I drank more, feeling wine-glow heating my veins. And something else: joy, love, surprise, what was it?

"Actually, I'm saving my facial hair in case I need an eyebrow transplant someday." He loves me, loves me not: I had giggles, not heartbreak.

She sucked in her breath and looked old. Her skin was pasty and unhealthy, mottled crepe at the neck. When was the last time she visited a doctor? I couldn't recall her ever going, but she must have, over the years. I only remember her working in the shop. Always working, making money to spend on me, her only child, ungrateful as ever.

"Okay, okay, you can fix me up sometime this week, I guess." I sighed and stood to refill her drink. She caught my hand as I reached for her glass.

"Is my little girl ready?" she said.

"Oh Lord, who knows?" I shook myself loose and went to get the bottles and heat up whatever food I could find in the fridge.

We settled in for a night of drinking and leftover lasagna instead of a nice dinner out. I lit candles to make things festive. We had a wedding cancellation to celebrate, even if only one of us knew about it.

She grew teary talking of bingo strategy and Kyle's winning, and how her grandchildren would all be winners too. I became more clear-minded with each glass of wine. I'd travel, kiss the world one town at a time, not staying long enough to attach myself to land or people. My future would not be tethered to a husband, or long hours of menial work; something creative and new would spark deep inside me, and I would nurture that spark until it became a bright, sustaining flame. I refused to think about tomorrow, when it would be necessary to phone and notify and cancel.

"I wonder where he is," Mother said several times. I had stopped offering possible reasons, because I knew. But I didn't want to argue with her. Let the truth unfurl without me, I thought. She'll see.

Eventually, she moved to the couch and began to snore. I draped a blanket over her. As I removed her glasses, she murmured, "I just want things settled."

She meant me. She just wanted me sorted, slotted into a predetermined pathway. Could there be a worse outcome than a life without surprises? But I was moved by her single-mindedness. She thought she had my best interests at heart. She just didn't know them. Neither had I known, before.

"Try not to worry so much." I patted the top of her head and lay down on the small couch opposite. Strange, how we'd flipped positions on the marriage question. Would we ever see things the same way, be on the same side?

Staring at the ceiling, I sent love-waves to Kyle—detached fondness for a relationship that already seemed long past. I was grateful for what he'd given back to me without my even asking.

The shiny days before me were a gift I'd been too stupid to know I should want. It was a lucky break. I smiled myself to sleep.

In the morning rough fingertips stroked my neck.

"Allison," he said in a hoarse whisper that woke me instantly. My mother, across from me, blew bubbles in her sleep.

"Babe? What?" I reached for him. His body was familiar and warm. I felt the muscles of his shoulder and bicep working. He was jumpy, miserable, in fact. I could read that through his shirt.

"I don't deserve you." He bowed his head.

I squinted into the light streaming in and saw my free self, climbing a far-off mountain alone, heading away from me—roped to no one for safety, and without the slightest hint of hesitation. I wanted to throw that girl a lifeline before she disappeared.

"I panicked. I couldn't think, is all," he said.

I tried to look shocked, a little hurt, playing along. But it was like a balloon had popped in my chest and was whizzing around, blowing damp, stale air, yesterday's news.

"I made it as far as Sarnia and turned north. Don't even know which road I took there."

He picked up my hand and traced the lines of my palm.

"And then I hit the deer."

I nodded. Hangover nausea lapped at the edges of my esophagus, waiting for a chance to rise.

"That was my sign. The deer flew off the hood in pieces, like a strobe light flashing in the dark. It was in pieces, I swear. But when I pulled over to look, the deer wasn't broken up at all."

Surely it was dead, though. A terrible, ominous sign that we'd be foolish to ignore. My head pounded.

"Coffee?" I said.

"The money will give us our start. We'll buy a house, have kids right away. You can even go to college if you want."

I sank into the pillow. He wanted to go back to Plan A. He

was being magnanimous, offering me something he thought only he could provide. A future boobytrapped with obligations. I must have been delusional with my night of fantasy freedom.

"When I saw that deer—" He shook his head. "I love you. Never doubt it."

"I know, babe," I said, closing my eyes. A rag doll would have more willpower than I did. "I know you do."

Me and Robin

"Who are you now, Robin?"

He pulls the long blonde wig over his crewcut and fixes the strands around his face. Then he tugs his jeans down below his hipbones, exposing a strip of white skin. The jump rope is the microphone, one wooden handle pressed into his lips as he puts on a show in our back laneway.

"I said, who are you?"

Robin stops dancing and opens his eyes. "I'm Avril Lavigne."

"Here, be Britney Spears." I put sunglasses on him and buckle him into the shiny pink bra stolen from our sister Katelyn's underwear drawer. He ties a turquoise beach towel around his waist and shimmies experimentally.

"Catch," I say, throwing the plastic doll to him.

"Baby." He hugs it close.

"Baby Sean. Take good care of him."

Tucking the doll under his arm, he shimmies some more, turning circles in the weeds at the edge of the pavement.

"How do I look?" he says.

"Girl, you look *good*!"

Robin smiles with such pure joy that I have to laugh at him. At him, not with him, but he can't tell the difference. For now, we're feeling up. We cut out of school this afternoon and no one's telling us what to do and even though it's fall, it feels like the ice cream truck will be driving up our street any minute, bell ringing. We both dance, singing and spinning until we fall down. It's hard to catch our breath for laughing.

"Krystal! Robin! Get home!"

"Mom," he says. By the dreamy look on his face, you'd think she was singing a lullaby, not shrieking our names up and down Alton Avenue.

"We're supposed to call her Linda, remember?" I reach for a stone and am pleased to see it fly a good distance down the lane that runs behind the houses on our block.

"Linda." His forehead is scrunched up. It's no use with that slow brain of his. I roll our things into the beach towel. We start toward home, not hurrying.

Personally, I couldn't care less what we call her. I may not be in high school like Katelyn, but eleven is old enough to understand some things. There's going to be a new baby—Linda says she's giving the mother game one more shot, with Troy this time. Tomorrow we're leaving our semi on Alton, moving to a bigger place farther out with cheaper rent. Still Toronto, but it might as well be Saskatchewan. I'll have to figure everything out again: the corner store, the streetcar stop, the laundromat, new people. School I've already figured out—it'll bite. My shadow-boy guarantees that.

We trudge down the lane, passing Joe and Elaine's backyard. Joe's bent over one of his cars, a paint-spattered rag hanging out of his pocket. He waves us over.

"Everything packed?" he calls.

"Nah, nothing's packed," I say. "She's freaking out."

Robin's fascinated by the rag. He reaches over to touch it, but I slap his hand away.

Joe doesn't mind. "Come see us before you go. Don't forget."

He's alright, that guy. Most of the people around here are alright, because this is a sweet place. Our street has swimming, skating, hanging around the park, whatever we want. We had a wading pool when I was little, until the city put in an icy splashpad that looks fun but isn't. They're building them everywhere, because you can't drown in a shower, can you? I heard about a girl last summer, though, the one who got her mouth stuck in the splashpad drain and ended up with bruised fish-lips. That's embarrassing.

We pass Anisa's yard, where a fence is slowly going up. Joe works on it Sundays, along with the old Korean guy whose house backs onto the lane across from Anisa's. He doesn't speak English, and Joe sure doesn't speak Korean, so they never talk. You see them working, handing each other tools and pointing, like mimes with no makeup. They must be psychic. Then Anisa will come out carrying drinks, and she'll talk loudly while they smile and sip. Anisa's long flowy dress reminds me of a jewel-coloured kite fluttering in the breeze. If she sees Robin and me, she'll insist on feeding us. She'll go on about her fence: the wood so free of knots, the perfectly straight posts, the privacy she'll soon have thanks to her excellent gentlemen neighbours.

"Chivalry lives, Krystal," she said not long ago, winking. "Contrary to our own experience with men."

Usually I have an answer for everything—just ask Linda. But that day I popped Anisa's funny sweets into my mouth and chewed like it was a full-time job.

"Have another ladoo," she said. "*You* certainly won't get fat." She sighed over the plate of golden yellow balls but didn't take a second one herself.

We get to our own back fence. There's no gate, but it's no

problem because we've bent permanent toeholds in the chain-link. As we go inside, Robin bangs the screen door into the lawn chair. It tips over, dumping a loaded ashtray onto the stoop.

"Idiot!" I say, before I can stop myself. He bites his lower lip, which makes me feel worse than if he fought back. Then he starts his hand-rubbing thing, which gets on my last nerve. He won't stop until he has something to hold, so I throw the beach towel at him.

Lately I think it's hopeless. I'm a year younger. A kid, not someone's mother and father rolled together. How am I supposed to protect him all day long from the ones who want to chase after him and yell *fag*? And there's a lot worse out there; I see the news. Robin trusts everyone.

Inside the house, there's nowhere to sit. The living room is filled with boxes and piles of clothes. Linda stands over them, but she's watching her blaring TV show. She glances at us, then turns back to Montel Williams over in the corner. He's refereeing a shouting match between two stepmothers and the ungrateful girl they took turns raising.

"Where the hell have you kids been?" She looks like she's been crying again, but her puffy eyes could be water retention. Babies cause that.

"In the lane," I answer.

"Playing singer girls," Robin says, giggling.

Linda glares at me. "Why'd you let him do that?"

"Do what?"

"You know, act like a girl."

"It's just a game."

"He's not a little kid anymore. What if someone—"

"No one sees us in the lane, Linda. It's a hideout," I say, clearing space on the kitchen counter to make bologna sandwiches. "From you," I mutter under my breath.

"I'm not raising no lane-rats." She looks at Robin and frowns. "We'll be packing all night to get out of here."

"Where's Troy?" I ask.

"This isn't his junk."

Troy started dropping by last spring after Dad left to go out west. He and Dad drove delivery trucks together.

Troy doesn't pay attention to Robin. Which is a relief, because Dad never could stop. If he caught Robin playing with one of my dolls, he'd throw it away and make sure Robin saw him. I lost a good pair of patent-leather shoes that way, cute ones with sequins on the strap.

You know how they always say it's not the kids' fault when parents split up? That's crap. We know it was Robin's fault. Not that he did anything, but he was the reason. Dad said he didn't want any Barbie-boys. Linda fought for Robin back then, but now she doesn't know what to do with him, either. The special classes aren't making him any smarter, and he hasn't outgrown playing with girlie things yet.

I give Robin a sandwich and take one myself. Linda circles the room, picking up the odd item and throwing it into a box. Nothing seems to be more important than any other thing. We watch her and eat our sandwiches standing up.

In our room, there isn't so much to pack, but there's no point asking Robin to help.

"Want to play with my troll babies?" I say. "You can."

He nods happily and begins placing the trolls around his bed, grouping them into little troll families according to the colour of their whooshed-up hair.

I throw stuff into a box: perfume, my Avril CDs, and a few orange leaves from the park, not yet crumbling. Old *People* magazines, Linda's leftovers. A postcard from Dad, the only one he sent from British Columbia. It's creased from Robin holding it so much.

He falls asleep on the bed, and I pat the blanket around him. He murmurs, but no real words come. I throw the trolls into the box and write "R & K" on top in marker.

I'm not sleepy but there's nothing else to do, so I fish a magazine from the box, the one with Britney on the cover, and get into bed, too. Turning the pages, I read, once again, the short article tucked behind the cover story. I've almost memorized it: FIVE THINGS AVRIL HATES ABOUT BRITNEY. Number 1: she wears a bra as her top, out in public. The girl from Napanee wouldn't do that.

When I'm done reading, I get up and look out the window. The wind whips leaves around the back laneway as darkness slowly settles over and into everything: our street, our house, this room, our bodies, all washed away in the dark. I try to imagine the person who will be watching our lane from this very spot, after we leave tomorrow. But I can't decide if it's a boy or girl; I keep flipping back and forth. Maybe I should leave a note. Except what would it say—take care of our cracked patch of concrete? How lame is that?

Later, it's full night when I'm instantly awake, dripping sweat. 4:30 by the glowing alarm clock. I dreamed that we were swimming at Ashbridge's Bay. No one else was around. It was windy like November, and the water was really moving. We counted to three and ran in, splashing and freezing and laughing. But then Robin's hands were tangled in my hair as we scraped the sandy bottom, our legs scissoring the water. I couldn't swim to the surface. He was too big to carry that way.

I take deep breaths and try to calm down. Too bad I woke up so soon. Someone might have been coming to rescue us.

My eyes are still adjusting to the darkness. I have to look at Robin's bed twice before I realize it's empty. The wig is spread across his pillow. The doll is next to it, swaddled in the beach towel, face down. And he's not there.

Shit, he's always there.

I walk downstairs, flip the basement light on, and worry for a moment about the centipedes. But down I go anyway, then right back upstairs to check the other bedrooms. Katelyn is snoring, mouth wide open. Robin is nowhere.

I open Linda's door and listen.

"Robin?"

Linda rolls over. Troy is up on his elbow, squinting. "What?" he says. "*What?*" as if I've been bugging them all night.

"Robin's gone."

"He can't be."

"He is."

"Go away."

"But—"

"Whatever it is can wait until morning."

"Linda," I say, louder now.

"Out."

I slam the door and walk away. Linda mumbles, and Troy shushes her gently.

My throat aches from fighting tears, but part of me is numb. The part that kept hoping we could be a normal family, with parents who decide things.

Back in our bedroom I unwrap the baby doll and hold him close. Then I put the wig on his bald head. I stroke the long strands, pulling them around the body. The wig smells musty, but it will keep the chill off.

Nothing is clear out in the laneway except the watery circle of yellow around the streetlight. For one odd second I feel a flicker of relief: Robin's left home and that's the end of it, goodbye. I'm so tired. But then shame rushes in with fear right behind it. He's out there crouched in some shadowy corner, shivering and scared.

All I want is to fall into Robin's messy sheets and cry my own storm. But I have to go out looking. There's no other way.

I scrabble in the shoe pile and jam my bare feet into a pair of runners before slamming the door hard to warn whatever might be outside that I'm coming. I haven't got a clue where to start looking but head toward the lights on Dundas. It's creepy without traffic, too quiet.

I play out possibilities. Robin wandering the streets lost. Someone jumping him for money, or for something worse. Hit by a car. No pleasant choices spring to mind.

I jump when a skinny guy in a leather jacket turns off a side street. He keeps on walking, but calls, "Get home, babygirl," as he passes by. When I turn to make sure he's gone, the first silver light is streaking the grey sky behind me. This day is coming fast, like all days that you dread. Moving Day, hooray.

Bautiste Convenience is open all night and there's Mr. Bautiste himself, sitting behind the counter reading the *Sun*. He smiles—wide, genuine—and doesn't seem surprised to see me. I can almost feel his summer warmth reaching me in the cold doorway, the welcoming warmth his kids bask in every day of the year. "My beauty-of-dawn, shouldn't you be home in bed?"

I hug myself, wishing I could hide my wrinkled PJs.

"I'm looking for my brother," I say. "Robin. You know?"

Frowning, he grabs a fistful of bubblegum from the jar on the counter and comes to stand with me. He takes my hand and gently presses my fingers around the gum. "Have you tried the park?" he asks. "I think he likes the park very much."

I nod, afraid I will cry, but manage to whisper, "Thanks, Mr. B."

I cut back, jogging. The park seems to be pushing up out of the misty shadows: the ball fields snugged up to Greenwood Avenue, the empty playground, the dog-running area where owners yell "he's friendly" at each other like the words are a magic charm. On our side of the park, grandmothers stand in the wet grass, doing their Tai Chi. They move together slowly as if following silent orders. They could be dancers floating through water. I want to float along with them, melt into their changing shape, and forget about everything.

But I can't see Robin anywhere. Even though the air is fresh and sharp, my chest feels tight. One of the Tai Chi ladies breaks formation, looks at me, and points north, toward the pool. She jabs her finger in the air several times as if to say *go that way, go now.* Her lips are curved in an imitation of happy. I feel like I could almost hug her, but instead I just nod that I got her message and run in the direction she showed me.

The pool hasn't been drained yet; the water is glassy and still smells of chlorine. We were swimming here last week. Thousands of kids splashed around us, but we didn't play their games. We stayed together.

I circle behind the change rooms to the path, where you can watch swimmers through the broken places in the tall, slatted fence. A sagging concrete wall is pushed into the hillside along the path, overgrown with weeds and scrub trees. Shards of glass and garbage are scattered around.

I stop short when I see him.

Robin is sitting on the wall, staring at the pool, legs dangling. His eyes are sleepy, kind of dazed. He doesn't look afraid, but empty somehow. He turns toward me, and I see a line of dried blood running from his eyebrow down to his cheekbone. His shirt is ripped at the shoulder.

Every part of me is shaking from the morning chill or leftover panic or relief; I'm not sure which. I rub my hands together, try to get a grip.

Finding my brother this way, seeing his skinny body again, it hits me all at once how he's mine. My problem that will never go away, even when we're grown-ups. It's like someone lighting a match in my gut; I wrap my arms around my middle and hold on until I feel stronger.

Who knows why I was the one chosen for him? No one else, just me. It makes no sense. He needs someone stronger. But now I get it: I'm choosing him, too. I could sneak away, but I never will.

· "What are you doing, Robin? Did you fall down?" I reach out to touch his cheek, which is swelling up, but he tilts back out of my reach. "That doesn't look deep. It'll heal in no time."

He grabs my hand and looks at me hard, like he's trying to figure something out. Then he gives up.

"I want to swim. Swim, swim, swimming," he says in singsong, head bobbing in a way that reminds me of him twirling around the lane.

I pull him off the wall, shaking my head no. "Let's get out of here. No one knows where you are."

He squeezes my hand and tugs, his eyes pleading.

I look at the water and shiver. Then I smile at him, and he giggles.

Cold and stupid, that's what this is. I can't think about getting caught. It won't matter anyway, after we move.

We strip down to our underwear and charge the fence. We're over the top fast and quiet, the way spies would do it.

"Who are we?" Robin says as we climb down the other side.

"Soldiers," I say. "Let's be soldiers."

He nods and crouches low, aiming his pretend rifle from side to side, looking for the enemy. We inch forward. At the edge of the pool we whisper-count to three and jump, holding in our screams.

Just before hitting the water I think of the Tai Chi ladies surprised by splashing sounds. I know they'll creep closer to check on us, our silent army buddies on the move. Together they'll glide into a new position and cover us until we're standing outside the fence again.

Masters Swim

400 m warm-up (swim/kick x 100)

Marta slipped into the fast lane, breaking the surface with a subdued *plomp*. Her arms flew up, then fell. They did not sync with the music blaring from loudspeakers, would not obey the propulsive beat. She had the ability to isolate herself. Overhead, a string of pennants fluttered like Buddhist prayer flags in the wind of giant ceiling fans. Beyond the fans, a fretwork of ducts and pipes mapped the indoor sky for backstrokers trying to stay on course. Her backstroke was uncertain, but she preferred its view to the endless black line on the bottom of the pool, and it gave her eyes a rest from the mural on the far wall, a garish beach scene two storeys high. Sometimes she flipped over and floated just to study the ceiling's layered shadows. How she might render them in charcoal on paper. If she could.

Saturday-morning swimmers emerged from locker rooms

into the chlorinated pool air, goggles in hand. They paused when the music hit them. Turn it off, Marta sang under her breath, but there was no chance of that. Lifeguards and swim instructors danced in place, causing the flotation devices slung across their bodies to jiggle. Teenagers shaking butts and wrists, cracking each other up. No more than five years separated Marta and the oldest lifeguard, but they were crucial years. At twenty-six, she felt ancient in comparison.

Too early for this. All night she had worried the sheets on Jill's pullout sofa, where she'd landed after abandoning California. The dream of art school lost, and with it the money she'd saved working retail. Not only working, but hesitating, never feeling ready. Jill had raced through college on a scholarship while Marta floundered. And then she stayed too long, but the faith that California might yet have something vital to offer had pinned her in place.

Marta closed her eyes and sank. Hugging herself, she felt in her element. How easily the water claimed her. She was still astonished at finding a welcoming space in this strange combination of sport and meditation. Soon after venturing into the pool at the Y, she'd advanced from floating half-laps to an hour, sometimes more, of steady movement. Swimming was the one thing that silenced *now what?*—her unwanted mantra. She could rinse her brain. And she expected that this was not only a California thing, but true of any pool. She lingered under water, slept for the span of a held breath, before rising again.

Bouncing in her corner, warmer now, Marta surveyed the benches lining the walls. She'd expected Jill to beat her here. Perhaps her younger sister had been waylaid by a friend, one of the crowd that cheered whenever Jill leapt into a new adventure, this time as entrepreneur. Marta batted the still water. She hoped Jill hadn't invited anyone. She'd agreed to test Jill's prototype, but that didn't mean she wanted an audience.

As she stretched her shoulders, Jill appeared at the far doors, balanced on crutches. Wearing a sundress that grazed her calf-high cast, burdened by a backpack, she manoeuvred past girl lifeguards bumping hips, rounded the corner at a clip, and continued the length of the pool. Marta gasped. The tile was wet, the rubber crutch tips smooth, Jill's expression determined. Safely reaching the bench closest to Marta, she sat. Shrugging off the backpack, she strewed the bench with possessions: a notepad, pen, laptop computer, phone, and several versions of the prototype swim mask, rubbery mounds she untangled and spread as though smoothing the frowns from children's faces. The mask was her child. She'd distilled her passion for excellence into an irresistible product that would revolutionize the sporting goods market. That's exactly how Jill had put it when she'd called from across the continent, startling Marta into a snorting laugh she tried to muffle, but Jill carried on, not hearing or choosing not to hear. Later, Marta read the same sentence on Jill's website, hyping a future success she took for granted. Which somehow produced success, a circular, proven mystery. Marta didn't doubt fortune would favour her sister once again.

Perched on the bench, Jill made a cheerleader megaphone with her hands. "Hey-hey, what do you say?" She tilted her head toward the lifeguards, then toward Marta. "Represent, sistah!"

"Really?" Marta mouthed. The lifeguards paid no attention to Jill's contribution to the din.

"It's showtime." Jill performed an air breaststroke, swaying her upper body in time with the music. Marta eased her goggles into place, pressing to ensure a good seal. Consulting the blackboard for instructions, she was pleased to see the Masters workout from last night's practice had not yet been erased. A rest day was prescribed, but Marta needed laps. She'd do the whole workout again, by herself.

Backstroke to start, following the pipes in the ceiling,

meditating on the little flags, which had no choice but to endure the breeze. Calm, accepting strokes. Then 100 kick with flutter-board, 100 breast, 100 kick again: sixteen easy lengths.

400 pull (3/5 breathing pattern x 100)

Panting, she stood at the wall, squeezing water from her pony-tail. She pushed the goggles to her forehead and met Jill's frown.

"What?"

"Why are you using those? You're wrecking your skin. The test won't be accurate."

"Habit? I can't swim without goggles; the chlorine is killer here."

Jill grabbed her phone and held it out, snapping photos. "We'll document the damage then. Puffy pouches, unsightly lines. Don't worry, not smiling is *perfect*—this is the 'before' picture." She checked her shots, selected one, and typed with her thumbs.

"Say goodbye to racoon eyes for-evah! Testing skin-like SKoggles today. Hashtag no wrinkles." She looked at Marta. "What do you think?"

"You've already posted, so why ask me? But you're not supposed to take pictures in here." Marta pointed at the sign behind Jill, a bulleted list of commands.

"Whatever." Jill twisted around to photograph the sign, narrating: "Making own rules to live by at hashtag SKoggles hashtag freedom."

"They're watching you." Two boys and a girl in red lifeguard shirts caucused by the defibrillator without appearing to take their eyes off the pool. "They're a credit to their training."

"They're just kids."

Marta replaced her goggles and reached into a bin by the side of the pool. She selected a foam wedge, placed it between her thighs, and pushed off the wall. When she made it to the end of the lane, she flip-turned and started back.

Jill yelled something, but Marta ignored her. She could see her sister waving when she breathed on the right side. Her breaths deepened and slowed as she dug for strength.

As Marta pulled, a bald and wiry young man wearing flippers slapped his way to the edge of the pool. Jordan, whose record times were etched on the plaque beneath the stop clock. His face grinned from a dozen photographs in Jill's apartment, appraising Marta as she cracked an egg in the frying pan or pulled the covers up to her chin or stepped into the shower. He wasn't grinning now, sitting with his feet hanging in the fast lane. He watched her progress for half a length before sliding in. He'd been dropping in to practise with Jill's Masters team while his shoulder healed. Marta was temporary. Not a competitor. He hadn't spoken to her yet, and if he'd stopped to speak to Jill on his way in, she'd missed it.

He dunked himself and affixed his goggles. She dove beneath the rope and swam in the medium lane, farther from Jill. He spread his arms for a showy butterfly stroke, loud and powerful. She pulled against his residual waves, slowing.

16 x 25 w/ :10 rest (1 fast, 1 EZ)

Resting against the wall, she removed her goggles and left them poolside next to Jordan's flippers. He was eating up the fast lane, lap after lap. She caught Jill watching Jordan with a haughty smile, as if she found his exertions amusing rather than impressive. She was following his progress too avidly for someone who claimed to be over him. Marta had to shout to get her attention.

"Ready!"

Jill hobbled to the edge of the pool without the crutches, holding one of the prototypes. Grabbing the ladder, she dangled the mask, preparing to toss it to Marta. Jordan powered in and executed a flip-turn that sprayed three lanes. Jill hopped backwards and cursed. He was halfway to the other end before she regained her balance. A stricken look flashed across her face, and Marta softened, wishing she could protect her younger sister, who so rarely needed protection. She ducked under the lane rope and came over, wincing at the sight of Jill's purple toes beneath the plaster.

"You should put a bag over that cast."

"I'll take my chances." She sounded upbeat.

Willed optimism, was that her secret? True to form, Jill had mastered whatever pain came from seeing Jordan and was once again hyper-focussed on her creation.

"Wish I could swim. I'm dying to test the mask myself."

"No more drunk breakdancing, then," Marta said, quoting Jill's defiant code phrase for her final date with Jordan, a night of dancing followed by a car accident that injured them both. "Hope you've learned your lesson."

"Ha, right." Jill paused. "Marta," she began, and fell silent. She focussed on the mural across the pool.

"Yes?"

"I just want you to know how glad I am that you're here. I mean that. And even if I could swim right now, I'd still choose you to test my masks. Because this is a big moment, and I want to share it with you."

Marta tried to open her expression. She wanted to be grateful for a sisterly confidence, whether sincere or an act of charity. She wished she could say the right, loving thing in response, but all she could manage was to join Jill in studying the awful mural. The scale was wrong. A giant toddler poked his plastic shovel into a sandcastle taller than he was, a leaning tower about to collapse and asphyxiate him. A pigtailed girl snorkelled amidst unlikely fish, her nose bulbous beneath the mask. Marta mentally repainted the nose.

"I don't really know what I'm saying," Jill said.

"I get it. You don't mind my couch-surfing. You want me to move in permanently."

"Ha."

Jill raised her prototype in both hands. "Here's to a fabulous launch, a major milestone in my company's success."

"Alright, give it to me."

Reaching for it, she brushed Jill's fingers, transmitting a flash memory: cottage summers, shrieking girls on a madly tilting dock, pushing and pulling each other into the lake.

"What's funny?"

"Nothing." Marta wrapped the mask around her head and probed the thin covering, like saran wrap but more durable. She pulled the mask toward her upper lip, and it snapped against her skin. "Ouch!" She tugged more carefully. "That doesn't seem safe."

"So don't do that." Jill retreated to write in her notebook. Jordan approached in a storm of splashing. Marta shrank against the ladder to give him room.

Although the mask felt strange, it kept the swimmer's nose dry, and the skin-like profile offered no resistance. "Competitive swimmers shave their bodies to cut fractions of seconds off their times," Jill had texted Marta while she was away at school. "They'll be all over this." Indeed, Jordan appeared to be completely hairless. Marta tried to picture him navigating the topography of ankles and knees with a razor. She herself had given it up as pointless.

In the medium lane, she alternated fast and relaxed lengths. During rests, she noticed swimmers watching her. There was a palpable lull in the activity; even the music had faded to an acoustic ballad. As Jordan rose from his completed lap, water sheeting from his smooth back, he didn't bother to hide his curiosity. In the seconds before he launched himself away, Marta fought an impulse to tear the mask from her head and hand it over the lane divider, the imprint of her features still fresh. Let a champion test the prototype. "*You* are the target market," she might say, by way of introduction. She could approach him. Just because she never was first to approach didn't mean it was impossible.

But Jill's plans for market domination went beyond competitive swimmers to aqua-fit ladies and anyone, really, who was concerned about appearances. Just yesterday she'd explained how this revelation came to her while she sat in the sauna, massaging the post-swim grooves around her eyes. Vacuum-sealing hard plastic to the delicate under-eye area had always bothered her. Ripping her goggles off time and again, she'd regretted the premature aging that would result.

"We willingly damage that fragile skin," she told Marta. "This product is a no-brainer. We can sell it with sporting goods *and* anti-aging products."

We? As the weeks of Marta's stay edged toward a month, Jill seemed to be incorporating her into the business plan. Employee number one. Marta felt a spasm of negation. She remembered their mother's admonition: *When you visit your sister, don't treat her like an Airbnb.* "What does that even mean?" she'd replied, thinking, I'm the one you should be worried about. But she hadn't shared any details of the depression that clawed her down, the anxious thoughts stalking her. *Now what* for Marta after her odd breakdown?

Pausing to rest again, she said, "It feels a bit claustrophobic. Like those cut-off stockings Mom made us wear at the cottage to protect against blackflies, remember? Nose and eyes flattened. Is that how I look?"

"You look fierce," Jill said, taking another photo. She swiped the image. "Making history with hashtag SKoggles test—you saw it here first, people. Smooth skin forever."

The masks were made of latex exercise bands that Jill bought in bulk and repurposed with a glue gun and ingenuity. Each green, red, or purple band featured a translucent plastic eye-shield in the centre, a one-way ventilation membrane over the nose, and Velcro strips for an adjustable fit—handmade for now, but the search for a manufacturer was on. She'd applied for a patent and contacted angel investors.

Jill had begun developing the mask last fall as a sideline, since her sales job wasn't challenging. Marta had just left for the renowned San Jose art program, where she discovered that she was unable to produce anything but panic for studio courses in painting and sculpture. She perceived her lack of talent in brutal peer critiques; in the way her sculpture professor would rearrange his face before pronouncing his verdict on her attempts to make art: humdrum, not up to the San Jose stan-dard. Whatever that was—she never figured it out. As she failed, Jill's long-distance invention updates fell like paint splatters. Marta couldn't think or eat or sleep. An interval exploring the ashrams and temples of the West Coast followed, during which Jill's messages went unread, and then measured days of swim-ming and solitude. By the time Marta dragged herself east for a summer of recalibration, she found the prototype ready to launch, its creator in a cast but undaunted.

Squinting, she saw that the lifeguards were transfixed by her head, as though a superhero had entered their midst. The chief lifeguard, surveying the pool from his tower, momentarily ceased his side-to-side scanning. Jordan glanced over between laps. She was a freakshow. Maybe she wouldn't do the whole workout today; screw that.

A group of kids and mothers in bathing suits and towels

trooped hand-in-hand from the family change room, heading for the wading pool. As they passed, a small boy pulled free, pointing at Marta. His mother stopped, sending a ripple through the chain. The boy's older brother yelled, "Voldemort!" as the younger child wailed.

"Shoo," Jill said, although Marta couldn't tell whether Jill meant her or the kids.

"Here goes," Marta said, and began a fast front crawl.

4 x 125 w/ :30 rest (25 sprint, 100 smooth)

Marta gained speed, a surge of energy propelling her wall to wall. Had she ever swum this powerfully? There was little difference between the first length, sprinting, and the four smooth ones that followed.

After two sets, she switched into the fast lane with Jordan. A ripple of irritation flowed between them, but maybe she was projecting. During Masters practices, swimmers shared lanes by staggering themselves. Jordan should be able to tolerate a single swimmer who took up less space than the average guy. He passed her, steaming ahead with ultra-productive strokes and kicks. He didn't seem to be favouring the shoulder. So unfair, the lightness of his injury compared with Jill's cast. He'd been driving that night.

She fell back, momentarily increasing the distance between them, but then caught herself. This was false courtesy, habitual deference that no longer served her. She had a right to be here. She tasked herself with catching him and almost did it. As he pushed off the wall, she glimpsed his face, startled at finding her in the shadow of his flip-turn. She swam the rest of the set trailing close behind.

On the last length, he opened a gap and then stood at the

wall, waiting for her. As she glided in, he looked her over, not just the mask, but up and down. She held the edge of the pool, breathing hard.

"What the fuck, did I miss Halloween?" he said.

She turned away and shook her head to release drops from her ears.

From the sidelines, Jill wanted in. "How does it feel?" she called. Marta imagined the two of them together: on the dance floor, in bed, on the roadside after the accident, which they blamed each other for. He had been around while Jill was developing the masks. She refused to believe this was his first time seeing one—anyone in Jill's orbit would have seen them. He was just being a dick. Unwrapping the back with a rip of Velcro, she pulled it tighter and gave Jill a thumbs-up public vote of confidence.

"Awesome."

Jordan, squinting at the diving board, said to no one, "Awesome. Fucking A."

Jill clapped. "Yay! Keep going—stretch it, test it. We need to find the weaknesses."

Jordan lowered his head, tucked his legs against the wall, and pushed into a backstroke that carried him away.

The chief lifeguard stared at Marta and Jill, whistle clamped in his teeth, and then resumed sweeping the pool for a life-saving opportunity.

4 x 75 pull w/ :15 rest (all strong)

Jordan kicked behind a flutterboard; Marta, pulling, managed to tail him. She surged, came close enough to touch his feet, and faded back. After several lengths like this, without making a decision to do so, her knees parted to release the foam wedge, which bobbed to the surface. She left it behind and was able to pass Jordan, noisily and laboriously stroking past him and his kickboard. He paused, treading water for a few seconds, before resuming his lap.

Pool etiquette dictated restraint, but she pressed onward, unable to stop herself. Never before had she harassed a person, much less someone she'd heard praised so much, until the breakup. It was like swimming was her drug, her oxygen. She forgot about Jill.

Jordan threw the kickboard onto the deck, where it landed with a thunderous clap. The lifeguards swivelled toward the sound in unison. He began a mechanized, brutally efficient front crawl. It took her three lengths to catch him, and then it was possible only with careful timing of her departure: waiting for him to push off and immediately throwing herself into his wake. When she was in range, she extended a hand, brushed his leg, and recoiled at the strength of his kick. What if he struck her head? Her fingers tingled. When she reached the wall, a snap decision sent her back the way she had come instead of rounding to the other side of the lane. She swam against the pattern, and nobody died. She had to row herself sideways when Jordan showed up, almost hitting her head-on, but she kept going and he kept going, swimmers with different destinies.

He arrived at the end of the lane for the last time, vaulted from the pool, grabbed his flippers, and stomped toward the exit. Then he changed his mind and headed back, past Marta in the pool and Jill on the bench, to the window of the lifeguards' office.

"Marta," Jill said, "what are you doing?" but Marta was watching Jordan. He jabbed the counter as he talked, his stance spring-loaded, like a sprinter on the starting block.

She registered the pair of lifeguards approaching Jill. Tall and short, both blond with freckles, the head guard and a younger one, less sure of himself. They could be brothers. Jill crossed her arms, thrust her jaw. Marta felt sorry for those kids, not realizing they stood no chance.

Jordan walked the long way around the pool toward the change room. As he passed the first aid kit mounted on the wall, he whacked the metal box, producing a loud clang. The mothers in the wading pool grabbed little arms and angled their heads toward the threat, alert as deer. When the echo faded, they let go.

300 swim free, smooth perfect technique

Marta swam her lengths, forgetting about Jill and the lifeguards. She revelled in the disappearing act of counting metres, the increasing number a kind of chant. She aimed for a focus point beyond which thought softened around the breath, open and inward at the same time. Without losing the number, she checked her time. Never had she been so clear-headed. So fast.

As she stroked without a hitch, she reflected on how different swimming felt with the mask on. For that was the source of her invincibility, surely. With an avatar, she gained power. Sleek SKoggles. She should suggest that Jill broaden her concept. Try the cosplay market, she'd say, and the notion made her laugh under water. But really, she ought to consider how this insight might apply to life outside the pool. She had painted masquerade scenes, the visual identity gag. What would happen if she somehow escaped her public self? Was it simply a matter of crafting a persona and boldly inhabiting it, or was an actual change in appearance necessary? A hat, hoodie, or scarf, a burqa. Arm over arm, Marta crawled without intention; breathed without worrying about when the next breath would come, her technique smooth.

Rounding a turn, she saw Jill gathering her belongings with exaggerated precision. She seemed to be searching for something but perhaps was stalling. The lifeguards hovered nearby, and now they were waiting at the end of the lane. Waiting for Marta to stop.

She lifted her head. She knew the suspended moment before the lap period ended, when swimmers were not quite finished, and the lifeguards itched to get them out. They'd push the oversized metal caddy closer, play with the hooks where the lane markers were secured to the pool wall, and start rolling up the lanes anyway, cranking the handle. The most tenacious ignored the signals. A nod indicated that you were leaving in a minute. You'd be out before the next group claimed the pool, after another length, just one more, one last …

100 choice cool down

The head lifeguard knelt at the end of the lane. Marta was about to land right beneath him. He stuck a hand in the pool. She stopped.

Gulping air, she checked the clock and noticed the silence. Someone had turned the music off. Jordan stood on the deck, lurking. "There's another hour."

"Ma'am, you need to get out." The lifeguard's Adam's apple quivered. He exchanged a glance with his sidekick, who was standing.

"I don't understand." She compared the boys' noses and cheeks, noting the identical scatter of freckles.

"There's rules," the head guard said, pointing at the sign. "You're supposed to follow the—" He made a circle with his index finger.

"Sure, yeah," Marta said. "I got mixed up."

The younger guard squatted. "That's not all," he said. "We've had complaints about that—what you're wearing."

Marta glanced at Jill, who was on her way over, using the crutches. "A complaint? Or complaints?"

The first lifeguard cleared his throat. "That's an unapproved device. All equipment has to be approved."

"By whom?"

Jill pushed in, standing over the boys. "Where does it say that?"

"Policy. And that other complaint we talked about already."

Jill scowled at the wading pool. Three mothers had gathered their brood, swaddled in towels from neck to butt, to watch at a safe distance, mutely accusing. She raised her phone slowly.

The lifeguards both stood. "Ma'am, I'm going to have to ask you to leave," the older boy said.

The mothers pulled their children into a group embrace, shielding them. They shook their heads in disgust and gestured at Jill. She photographed them rebuking her.

The older lifeguard stepped between them. "I'm filing an incident report on this. You are barred from the premises for thirty days." Jill opened her mouth to argue, but nothing came out. Jordan took a step closer.

"And you," the lifeguard said to Marta. "That mask is scaring the children."

"This is *adult* lap swim, is it not?"

"Shh—" Jill hissed. "What are you saying, exactly?"

"Until it's approved, you can't use it here."

"What?" Jill stomped her cast and moaned in pain. Marta was glad she couldn't see Jordan, behind her, listening intently.

"I told you, policy," he said, shrugging. He and the younger boy left to give a report at the lifeguard window.

"Little dictators," Marta muttered.

Jill turned on her. "What's wrong with you? I do you a favour and you act crazy. Now you've damaged my brand. You managed to get my amazing"—her voice quivered—"product banned."

Marta sank to her chin. She opened her mouth, allowing a stream to flow in. The mask kept her nose dry, as advertised, and gave her an altered vision of her sister: a person who would always seek an adversary, creating one, if necessary. Opposition fuelled her.

"I thought you were getting your shit together." Jill pushed a kickboard into the pool with one crutch.

Marta ripped off the mask and let it float like a dead fish. She turned away from her sister to face the nightmare mural. Jordan, standing against a wall by the lifeguards' office, hovered at the periphery of her vision.

"Ugh, I can't talk to you. You're impossible." Jill spun on her crutches, passing Jordan on her way to the exit. As she neared the wading pool, someone catcalled, and she paused long enough to lift hand from crutch to give them the finger. A lifeguard stepped forward, brandishing a clipboard.

Marta looked at the mask just out of reach. Its development, approval, reception in the marketplace—none of this was her concern. She couldn't ruin Jill's plans any more than she could ensure Jill's triumph. Her actions didn't lead to clear outcomes; just look at the year she'd had. Attachment to outcomes was futile. Studying to be a painter didn't make one a painter. She needed to leave. She was already gone.

On the pool deck, Jill read what was on the clipboard but then brushed past the lifeguard, refusing to sign. Instead of leaving, she approached the diving board, lowered her backpack, and dropped the crutches. They hit the tile with the clatter of a miraculous cure.

Marta remembered Jill's extraordinary will as a child. At the cottage, she ruled the dock, despite being younger and smaller.

Marta would throw her overboard, thinking: victory! But the game wasn't over until Jill said so. She always got the last push.

Jill hopped one foot up the ladder, holding the rails. By the time the lifeguards got there, she was already on the board, inching forward with her arms out, the skirt of her dress swaying. No one climbed after her or tried to talk her down. Jordan didn't move.

Marta admired her balance. It took strength and mindfulness to stand lopsided on a diving board that flexed with every twitch. She covered her mouth when Jill bent her knees for a little bounce and almost fell sideways, pulled by the cast. At the second bounce, Marta retrieved the mask. Still watching Jill, she secured it around her head.

She missed the jump and the fall. She heard the shriek but had no chance to consider whether it was a sound of defiance or hurt, because she was already speeding toward her sister, guided by the instinct to rescue Jill from her first self-defeating impulse, an action that was never in the business plan. Or maybe it was the unfinished argument, the urge to shake Jill and be right, to have an opponent and pull her close. As Jill hit and sank, Marta gulped air and dove. Peering through the mask into the cloud of plaster around her sister, she swam downward as she had done a hundred times before to retrieve stones from the lake bed. She found Jill, scooped her under the arms, and pushed off from the floor. Jill tried to help with her arms and good leg. They made a cumbersome pair, as likely to work against each other as to find a rhythm. Marta knew the cast would slough off eventually, lightening their load, but she had no idea how long that might take. If it was anything like dissolving a hard edge of difference between sisters, they didn't have that much time. Her lungs burned with her last held breath. She tightened her grasp and kicked as hard as she could until slowly, together, they began to rise.

The New Kitten

Jamie shifts on her bank-teller stool, waiting while Mr. Ludder stacks change on the counter. A crabby customer with a quarter-million snoozing in low-interest accounts, he searches pockets for missed nickels. He prefers her to take his coin deposits, waving others ahead of him in the lineup until she flips on the light signalling she's free. She's never hit that switch without mentally reciting *free/someday free,* a fragment she's saving for one of her poems. A poem contrasting Tellers past, prim ladies trapped behind gilded bars, with today's Client Advisors, who work beneath the all-seeing gaze of ad-playing giant TV monitors, screens beyond Orwell's imagining.

During the micro-moments of transactions, Jamie thinks. Between ignoring the pop-up order to cross-sell a TFSA and printing the receipt, she scans the lobby for bank robbers, twitchy Tobias Wolff gunmen with no mercy for literary types. And sometimes she'll pick a Stephen Leacock character from the queue: the young rube clutching his $56 deposit, who'll be mortified no matter how kindly she treats him.

What she tries not to think about is her husband. Now that she knows about Todd's slush fund, the next move is hers, but what to do? He pushed her into this job, crying poor, yet hides a six-figure sum she discovered by accident, running address updates.

Learning they were rich—had been rich all along—was the wrong kind of epiphany. Moaning, she ran the report again. Bank figures don't lie, but people do. Where did the money in that account come from? What's he up to? Daily, she checks the account activity trying to figure out who he is.

Jamie's first day: the branch manager welcomed and oriented her, but it was big, brash Sadie who woke her up. When Maureen introduced her around, Sadie boomed, "You must be the new kitten."

Her co-workers, all women, tittered. She fought the urge to kick off her pumps and run; the tour continued.

"That's Sadie for you," Maureen said. "I expect you'll catch on. You've graduated university and now it's time for real-world schooling."

The new kitten—how to parse the phrase in a twenty-first-century workplace? Cuddly plaything; cute baby animal; sex kitten. Wrong on every level. And that was before she'd even met the grabby regional manager a month or so later. The other kittens failed to warn her about him, but one flesh-pressed "excuse *me*" as he slid past provided an instant education.

She followed Maureen around as if tailing the mother cat and returned home to a husband well pleased. He hadn't expected her to accept the entry-level job in financial services, her only offer.

"Vino for the victor," he said, holding up a wineglass. A muted proclamation, soft-pedalled to placate her. Todd was known as a top closer at his industrial equipment firm. "Not like grad school, is it, Jame." He feigned pity and kissed the top of her head, a kiss that praised results.

At first, she sucked at everything. She told herself English majors weren't meant to type strings of numbers with 100% accuracy. When people huffed about long lines, she tensed. And the analogue clients paying their bills in person, pushing sheaves of paper across the counter. She was supposed to shift them, gently, to online banking, but they resisted.

"Right, more fees," they said. "Highway robbery, no thanks."

Dealing with the public exhausted her.

"Why do I have to pretend the customer's always right?" she asked Todd. "They're idiots."

"C'mon, you're a rising star. I can totally see you fast-tracking to VP."

Why did he have to blow sunshine? Salesman of the year, that's why.

In the staff room, she forced herself to socialize instead of reading. Despite never having envisioned herself in a job like this, she wanted to fit in. The first week, Sadie pounced on Jamie's left hand, squeezing it between plump palms.

"Look at the *rock* on this gal. Caught yourself a winner, eh? What's hubby like?"

Everyone listened as she stammered that Todd was hardworking. That's all she had. Afterward, that pained her. And how backward the conversation was: marriage as currency, her face value.

Sadie's teeth flashed. "Hardworking in bed, sure." She'd

already overshared her history with Jamie: married twice, not making that mistake again. Her man visited weekends, the perfect amount of time. Jamie learned what he liked to do with Sadie, how often, which rooms. She didn't invite this information, but she didn't stop the flow, either.

Without Sadie, though, she would have quit. Once, converting American dollars, she became flustered. A woman rattled her keys as Jamie stared at the frozen screen.

Sadie reached over to rescue her. "This entry here," she murmured, typing. "Smiley face, honey."

Later, she said, "Rule number one: they're always watching."

"Security cameras? They're for our security, surely?" To stop a bullet in the brain, she added silently.

"Nah. They capture keystrokes, facial expressions, tone. Performance reviews, you get a list of deficiencies. Data from cameras and mystery shoppers."

"Who?"

"Paid spies who report whether you used their name three times, were you fast enough, did you cross-sell, up-sell."

"Side-sell," Jamie said.

"You got it. My advice? Memorize procedures cold, and you'll be fine. You're not the first kitten I've showed the ropes to. I trained Maureen, back in the day."

"Really?"

"And look how they promoted her over me."

Almost a year later, Jamie fits in, undeniably a favourite, especially after she planned a baby shower for Kerri, the Customer Care Coordinator. She organized food, decorations, and gifts, and she didn't flinch when Sadie said, in front of everyone, "We're waiting for you to get knocked up next, lil kitty."

Conception seems unlikely, given her flat-lined sex life. Since joining a bike club, Todd takes eight-hour Saturday rides with a crowd she's never met. Fun people, he says. Interesting and fit. Three high-end bicycles hang in their garage, and she happens to know, from studying his secret account, that he paid $3,000 for the cheapest one.

Closing her cash drawer at night, she counts bills, tallies the balance. Why is she the one worrying about what's gone wrong in their relationship? Why doesn't he?

Sadie fluffs her hair and sits at the next drawer over. Jamie gives her a wan half-smile.

Maybe she should join Todd's club. Shock therapy. How would she look in goggles and Lycra shorts with a padded butt? Like a bloated tropical bug. She'd rather be no fun.

"Got a romantic evening planned?"

She shakes her head, envisioning her welcoming books, Todd away again.

"You should follow the example of your elders." Sadie stands, shaking her hips. "David's coming this weekend. We're going to have so much *fun* rolling around."

Like Jamie needs to be confronted with gross middle-aged sex. Glancing at the poster-filled windows, she's startled to see her reflection superimposed on an advertisement showing joyful models caught mid-recreation—biking, hiking, planting flowers that will compound and grow. The cyclist resembles her husband; she hadn't noticed it before. He exudes Todd's bluster, smiling at the camera as if to indicate that he's such a good rider, he doesn't need to watch the road.

She scrolls through the transactions: bike shop, bike-trip lunches, normal stuff. Then, a meta-narrative in numbers. Charges from Vancouver when Todd said he was in Regina on business. Manhattan restaurants during the Winnipeg week. Florist, lingerie, liquor store, jeweller. She kills the screen. So banal, Todd's infidelity. So romance-novel. And he still has scads of cash.

Her new job affords more time to track him. With Kerri on mat leave, the branch needed an Acting Customer Care Coordinator, a position that comes with a glass-walled office.

Jamie's flattered that Maureen chose her for the role. Her less-experienced self might have missed the opportunity by indulging in wordplay—what about the Screwing the Customer Over Coordinator, is that job open? She held her tongue and was rewarded.

The office displays her like a museum specimen under glass, but she can swivel around, showing the back of her chair, while she talks on the phone to prospects. She swivels for difficult conversations.

Dialing his office, she tells herself it's just another cold call. *Cold* being the operative word. This will be an accounting, not a climactic scene of love and despair. She scans her memory for stories of wronged spouses and rejects the only one that comes to mind: the farmer stumbling into a prairie blizzard after seeing his wife and her lover, the paint on his hand an unanswerable message from the dead. Too subtle for this situation. She's alive, and she isn't in the mood for self-sacrifice.

"Todd Jennings."

Of course. He prides himself on answering his own phone.

"Hey there, it's your bank calling. We're smack in the middle of RRSP season and wanted to reach out. Looks like you have a substantial nest egg, a nice surplus to invest. Doing okay, but we can make that money work a lot harder for you."

"I—gee."

Such pleasure in hearing him fumble. He's never been good at voices, and she's out of context.

"Markets are rising. It's a good time to make a move."

"I hadn't really thought about—"

A screech penetrates the office. Jamie whips her chair around to face the lobby, where Sadie is storming around with raised fists, an opera singer howling at fate.

"That pig! You can't trust men!"

"Todd, can you hold please? Just a sec." She hits the red button, in control for once. She hasn't felt this good in a long time.

Sadie grabs brochures and throws them skyward. They litter the carpet. Customers step backwards but hold their place in line. And there's Mr. Ludder, patting his pockets obsessively, turning circles looking for her.

"I'm back. Where were we? Right: you hadn't really thought. About the money? Let's be real, it's your one true love. Oh, no doubt you have more than one love. A guy with your appetites. Why limit yourself?"

"Jame." A whisper.

Maureen hurries into the lobby and takes Sadie by the arm, leading her down the hall, followed by a security guard Jamie has never seen before. Has he always been lurking around, waiting for his moment to shine? Shrunken and spent, Sadie makes eye contact as they pass, and Jamie arranges her face in concerned solidarity, but Sadie's anguish is too much, too loud, and not, in the end, hers to accept. A clear and exhilarating vision overrides residual sorrow for her friend. Sadie made her choices, and she'll do the same.

She listens to silence on the line, patient, until Todd's breathing grows ragged. For a moment it moves her, but the feeling passes. This is how he wanted her: hard-edged, relentless. She knows how to close a deal too.

"I've got excellent suggestions for where to stick those funds! But here's what you do for starters: open two accounts and name one of them New Place to Live—"

"Are you going to let me explain?"

"The other, call it Hire A Lawyer. You need one."

She hangs up, satisfied to hear the disconnecting buzz. There's one more thing to do. She goes into the account and places an ironclad, fraud-alert hold on the funds. Brava. Afterwards, she drops head to desk, but she's dry-eyed, merely resting.

A knock on the door jolts her upright. Maureen appears, hair dishevelled and collar askew, pushing a young woman forward.

"Jamie, meet Susan. Remember, I told you she was starting today." Of all days, Maureen's widened eyes say. Help.

Crossing her arms, Jamie inspects the woman: bleached hair, piercings, manicure, but she could be anyone properly scared. "Well," she says finally, extending her hand, "you must be the new kitten."

Leaping Clear

She lay dozing in her sickbed when the boy came to rumple her thoughts. Not the one she shotgun-married in her petrified youth. It was the summer boy from the city. Jackson, who left in a cloud of dust, the doomsaying of his people and hers blowing hot at his back. It was his voice calling her name. *Kathleen*—first a whisper and then louder, waking her.

Afternoon light sliced through the blinds, gilding her bedroom, and seeing familiar objects mystically glowing made her love them anew: the worn cotton coverlet, white with a band of light blue stripes, pulled tight across John's side of the bed as it had been for the last two decades; her walker propped next to the bed, with its quilted hanging pockets holding eyeglasses and magazines; the knotty pine floorboards, sloping downward from the window toward the centre of the old house; the maple dresser lined with prescription bottles alongside the statue of the Virgin Mary strung with rosary beads and the brass crucifix her parents had given them for a wedding gift; the rocking chair where she used to sing her babies to sleep. And now Jackson, somehow here, what on earth?

He stood next to her bed with hands in his pockets, looking reproachful but also amused, because he already knew her story and was free of it. That's what she believed, anyway. He hadn't changed. He could have stepped out of the black and white photograph, the one of the group sitting thigh to thigh on the wagon at John's family's place, squinting into the late afternoon sun that glared down on them in godforsaken 1928, as in every year since.

Nights, she pulled it out of the album and turned it this way and that, the scalloped white border still sharp under her fingers. She smoothed the image, studying shades of grey for evidence. Her mind filled in the missing colours: blonde wisps of hair escaping from the red triangle of her scarf, tanned hands clasped primly while her whole body angled for him. His smart-aleck curved lips and deep brown eyes; the indigo dungarees, too new for him to be local. Seventeen and nineteen, glorious ignorance. You couldn't tell them a thing. He held an unlit cigarette in the air just above her shoulder, aimed at the road to town, and later she thought he'd been pointing toward the O&W line, the train that brought him and took him away again. He'd been sent upstate because his uncle needed farm help that season. His parents, having escaped the land themselves, thought it would be wholesome for young Jackson to touch dirt before taking up a position in the family firm. The picture was her prayer, her search for signs. Signs were as hard to catch hold of as lightning—flashing while her eyes strained to see patterns of meaning; burning when they hit ground.

"Why didn't you come?" he said.

He squatted against the wall, bouncing lightly on his heels. She took in his yellow chambray shirt, the dungarees. The shock of him. How she had longed to see his face, day upon day. But she could not have predicted that someday he'd appear unaltered, undimmed in any aspect, to gaze on a decrepit version of herself. A flicker of shame passed through her, although there was nothing to be done about old age. It had happened to her and not to him, simple as that.

"Were you there?" The fear of that time returned as a feeling of iciness, crystals growing in the region of her lungs. She had to remind herself that breathing was required to continue this conversation. Breathe, it was so long ago.

"I waited at the station in Weehawken. I brought a ring." His tone was flat. She interpreted this to mean that any anger or sorrow he had once harboured had long since leeched away, an enviable state of mind she had not achieved. "You didn't trust me."

"It wasn't—I—" Her voice failed.

What had happened after Jackson left? She'd told and retold the tale to herself, but the true story wouldn't find purchase in her memory. She was always changing this or that, little details that never shifted the ending.

He left in a hurry. Her family's grip tightened. They held her in place; that much was true.

Jackson's father had received reports of his son and the neighbour girl meeting in the woods and acted quickly. Jackson was summoned home.

The reports were accurate. Shortly after meeting Jackson at a social, Kathleen offered to show him the trail that led to Busfield's pond, and the cool, wet caves beyond, and, even farther, following a narrow path up the hillside, the lookout over the Delaware River. The trail passed behind her house and Jackson's uncle's property before veering across the railroad tracks, through a dense spruce grove, to the pond. Their secret places, their disappearances.

If she were to rise from her bed, walk to the window, and lift the blinds, she'd see the trail in the distance, although it, like everything else, had changed in the intervening years. Instead of a rough path beaten into the land by the feet of children running beyond earshot of adults, it was now a proper trail, graded and covered in fine stone screenings, maintained by the town, marked by benches and interpretive signs. The old rail bed, long abandoned, had been groomed into another intersecting trail. And the people had changed. Today's walkers wanted fitness; they took big strides in expensive footwear, swinging ridiculous ski poles, which, her son informed her, increased the heart rate. Working themselves up on purpose. They didn't know any better, she supposed, never having experienced either physical labour or natural, seasonal rhythms of rest. They wouldn't understand the concept of meandering past cedars and ferns, the shadows and the clearings, being at home there. The freedom of stepping into the woods, alone or with a companion, with no clear purpose. As she had done many times, before and after Jackson.

He had been forced to leave. Her parents were so thankful to be rescued that they chose not to brood about the insult. Catholic farmers and Protestant bankers were agreed on the subject of oil and water, if nothing else.

But before any of that happened, rumblings. Mealtimes larded with lessons. Even in her hazy lovestruck state, Kathleen understood. Dad would pause, holding his spoonful of soup mid-air for a moment of reverence before saying what it symbolized.

"We mayn't have much, but loyalty to your own is a thing beyond price." He'd look around his table, from little Marie blowing bubbles in her bowl, to the boys nodding earnestly, to Kathleen, the eldest, with her head bowed, to their mother, sharp-eyed.

"You children keep that in mind."

Kathleen's mind couldn't help wandering to the clearing, well off the trail, where Jackson pulled her down with him into the tall tickling grass, laughing and warm, stroking the length of her hair with one hand while the other roamed freely over her skin.

"We never took the Prot soup back then," Dad would say, slurping his. "Even when we were over there starving for it. We kept the faith."

"That we did." Mom knew her lines. There was no need to elaborate further on the ancient, yet always fresh, outrage of the soup offered to famine-scourged Irish Catholics in exchange for their conversion. The potato famine an inherited grievance. Lost to living memory, but they kept it alive through recitation.

Then she'd see her chance to mention a scrap of news from the radio, an outbreak of food poisoning at a restaurant, or a confidence game the police had put a stop to. The city was full of people ready to prey on the virtuous. Their life close to nature couldn't be beat for love or money.

"What can you expect but food poisoning, eating caviar and such?" She'd wrinkle her nose and take a bite of boiled potato.

Kathleen heard the warnings against uppityness, vanity, the deadly sin of pride—above all, against outsiders. But they were distant church bells muted by a fog of love and something else, a newfound rebellion that shook her. She never replied. She'd hurry to clear the table, turning away so they couldn't see her face and guess. Protestant or Catholic, what did it matter? She meant to leap clear of all that dead history. She began to see her parents as shrunken seedpods holding the beliefs of a century ago, a country ago. She wished for a strong wind to scatter their contents on the rocky ridges that plagued their land, where they would shrivel and die.

And then the morning Jackson called in. That last day, just before his hot and dry walk into town to catch the return train. He stood for a moment in the doorway, not invited to come in and sit down, but still somehow pushing himself forward in that polished manner that got him what he wanted.

Dad, hesitating, gave way while Jackson walked in, but he stood with his hand on the door.

"Yes?" he said. Kathleen stood behind him, sneaking glances at Jackson. His face solemn, a mask of respect holding his features in check. Sweat dripped between her breasts.

"I'm going home today," Jackson said, and then greeted Mom, hovering in the background. "Mrs. O'Donnell."

Kathleen felt frozen in place, seeing Dad's hand drop off the door, hearing her mother's quick intake of breath, but unable to move or speak herself. It couldn't be true.

"It's for the best, surely," said Dad.

"Goodbye, Kathleen. Maybe you could write me some time," he said, attempting a smile while Dad recovered himself and frowned at her, shaking his head ever so slightly.

She nodded anyway, tears forming but not yet coursing down her cheeks.

They wouldn't have another second alone. No private goodbye or figuring what would come next. But he must have expected that. He was smart about things.

He stepped forward with his hand outstretched and they shook like strangers saying pleased to meet you, while he pressed a folded square of paper into her hand.

Dad didn't extend his hand to Jackson and slammed the door after him, victorious. She stood there weeping, hands clenched, waiting for her chance to bolt. The full story was still to be read. But Dad believed, innocent as a child, that the closed door meant an ending of his choosing. And so, she wept for him too.

"Thank heaven that's finished," Mom had said, shooting her with a look that said carry on, girl; mind your dignity.

Jackson stood and approached her bedside. He touched her white hair and tucked a strand behind her ear. She remembered that he had once said her hair was as fine as corn silk. People said things like that back then; now it would be a bad joke, if anyone even understood it as a compliment. He leaned closer.

"Our folks would've come around," he said. "It could've been a grand time."

"You're forgetting the baby," she said and then wanted to claw her argument from the air. She pressed back into the pillow, turning her head fitfully. Perhaps death would come now to rescue her from her guilt. She was too tired to justify herself anymore.

"Yes, the baby changed everything, didn't it?" Jackson fixed her eyes with his, a small smile playing on his face as Kathleen moaned faintly. "Ivy, you see."

Kathleen closed her eyes to call to mind a picture of his pinch-mouthed cousin, dead now, like almost everyone she knew, which was the logical outcome of surviving ninety-three years. All the old neighbours, her parents, of course, and all but one of her siblings. She resisted feeling sorry for herself. It was a blessing she still had her son, who lived close enough to look in on her a few times a week, and this house that she grew up in, the O'Donnell homestead, or what was left to her after selling off fields and pastures over the years to people moving in from the city. The view from her front yard clotted with new houses, but the back was still open, grass and then garden and then the trail. She mostly looked out back now.

After Jackson left, Ivy mentioned him sparingly, as if ladling out the last of the well water. Kathleen recalled seeing her with a basket over her arm at Marino's Five and Dime, her darting eyes examining the child, her boy, while they chit-chatted about everything but the reason Kathleen spoke to her at all. They'd always been neighbours, in that sprawling country sense, and schoolmates. Never friends.

Chance meetings with Ivy yielded precious little: Jackson thriving in High Finance; Jackson the whirling beau of the ballroom;

Jackson linked to a girl from a prominent New York family. Drops from the kettle poured into cupped hands, enough to scald, no more.

And two years later, Ivy stood on Kathleen's verandah and spat at the tattered screened door, as though Kathleen were to blame for his jumping out the ninth-floor window of the Newsom Merchant Bank in faraway Manhattan. As though she had any connection to him at all.

Kathleen moaned again, feeling fresh pain that couldn't be tied to bodily function or geography. Just aching. The hopelessness of her position had seemed so clear then, but now it was hard to credit. Nowadays there'd be no risk, leaving all she knew to go after him in a blind rush, baby or no baby. His son.

The family danced around each other in the days after Jackson left. It was as if they had risen from their beds one day to find strangers eating at their table, without fathoming a meaning. Inside she was a mash of worry and trouble, fermenting with plans. But she was careful about her outside. She went around doing her chores, the dutiful daughter. She carried on.

As she secretly counted down the days left in August, she burned her parents' images into memory against the time when she would never see them again. Mom standing at the kitchen table, humming tunelessly through white-pressed lips as she sliced tomatoes for canning, dividing the skinned flesh from the seeds with her knife blade while juice pooled around her hands. Dad looking across the dinner table at her before standing abruptly, almost tipping his chair over. His look was pure appraisal. He knew about her condition, she felt it, yet he wouldn't or couldn't say the dreaded words.

She wished for better remembrances. Pictures that bespoke happier times, when she was content to take stock of the boys

overflowing their desks in the back row of the schoolroom, thinking *maybe him. Or him.* But wishes weren't going to save her.

As each day brought the rendezvous with Jackson closer, she
became less sure. She felt herself drooping like the parched cab-
bage plants in the garden, weighed down with heat.

And as the life hidden within her ripened, she began to tell herself bedtime stories with ruinous endings. The prodigal daughter
spurned at the farm gate, no hearts softening on her return. The
woman at the well, never meeting Jesus. The adulteress standing
before circling men, each perfectly willing to cast the first stone.

Worry wormed around her gut. What if Jackson wasn't there
to meet her? Where would she go? His family might stop him
from coming, or he might have changed his mind. The city was
full of suitable young ladies; never mind a poor country girl, a
Catholic no less, and with wrathful parents. She'd be destroyed
over a fairy tale, taken for a fool. She felt she could trust Jackson,
yet there was an edge of doubt. She had trouble imagining him
meeting her train; she couldn't picture the grand setting that the
Weehawken train station must be with the two of them in it, or
the ferry they'd take across the river to the terminal at the foot
of 42nd Street.

When John came calling, she was still flapping back and
forth like sheets on the clothesline, even though it was the night
before her city train. She heard him whistling and saw the sun
glinting off his blond hair as he strode toward the house. They
sat on the rough bench in the yard beneath the cedars, not saying much and yet comfortable together. She couldn't remember
a time when she hadn't known John. He grew up on a farm farther down the same county road. They had played together as
toddlers, studied at the same schoolhouse until he left to go to
work, laboured side by side in haying season when the families
put their horses and children together in the fields, and at the
last ceilidh of winter, they'd danced together.

She remembered that dance, the awkward way they bumped knees but laughed anyway as the fiddle music kept them bouncing. The bench creaked under his weight, and she thought he was as solid as they come. It was a shame that she'd never have his friendship anymore, once she got on that train heading toward Jackson.

He turned toward her and cleared his throat. "I seen how things was this summer," he said in a low tone. "And I see how things sit now."

She stiffened. She had caught him frowning at her at Busfield's pond, where the gang went to swim after sundown. Felt him watching even after she turned away. Everyone said John had no time for Jackson, the fancy-pants newcomer who didn't know anything. And since she had no time for anyone but Jackson, she'd ignored him.

"You and me, we're a pair," he said, looking at his dust-covered boots.

She softened then. He was waiting for her to say something, but what? And she thought: well, we could be a pair. She put her hand over his and squeezed it.

"Let's get married," he said, and then, as if feeling braver now that she hadn't stomped off and left him sitting alone, he smiled directly at her. "Marry me."

And so it was that she settled for being saved by John, after Jackson had cleared out but before she'd anywhere near recovered. She leaned into him and allowed him to rescue her, a lifetime bargain they never spoke of.

Mulling it over now, she marvelled that she and John had left so much unsaid. But it was well before the time when people started sloshing their feelings all over the place.

"You didn't have faith in me," Jackson said.

Yes, it was definitely better the old-fashioned way. What was the use of going over the past with a fine-tooth comb? There are bound to be some nits.

She turned on her side and choked on the ice spreading up to her throat. "If it's faith you're after, maybe you could explain how … Ivy told me—she couldn't wait to tell me." She whispered to the wall. "How could you destroy yourself? Was it because I didn't come?"

He didn't answer. The first birdsong of the day trilled outside the window, and still he was silent. She nodded, reinforcing herself. She could ask questions.

"Why have you come back now?" she said, setting her mouth in a tight line. And then she thought she knew why. She turned back to face him, but he'd ducked out of sight, just like before.

The marriage started slowly, though love gained ground over time. She promised herself that first year to put Jackson behind her, but it proved harder than she had thought. The doubts that had plagued her in August gradually hardened into a certainty that the life she'd missed was a life of ease, full of beauty and laughter. She had chosen badly, she came to see.

The baby was born in early April, a sturdy boy with a head of black hair. They named him Thomas, after John's father. No one mentioned Thomas's dark eyes or premature arrival.

Their families helped them set up house nearby in their first place, a rental with acreage, but crop prices had fallen so low it was hardly worth harvesting, so John found work at the silk mill in town. He came home with fine cuts all over his hands and a dry cough that would never leave him be.

Shortly afterward, the stock market crashed, and then the mill closed. They scraped through the winter after that, John rattling around the sheds, never finishing jobs that he started.

He doted on Thomas, though. That was a blessing.

"Circus strong man," John would say with a wry smile as Thomas grabbed his dirt-scratched thumb and held on, laughing from the gut. "Tough guy."

But nights could find him standing at the window, just looking. Once she woke to see his face in pure moonlight, pale with fear and resignation. She marked his sorrow and knew she was powerless to help in any way; she could even be the cause of it. The only certainty was that he wouldn't tell if asked. Jackson, she was certain, would have talked with her as a pal, would have joked away the worst hardships. He had so liked to talk and laugh.

Then she fell into a sleep marred by twisted dreams, lying in a green pasture, her head in Jackson's lap. He smiled down on her, gently teasing her hair into a fan around her face, rubbing her temples, soothing her. He began to pour something from a cup held high above her. He poured with a flourish, back and forth to wet all the hair, and she thought that this is how it must feel to be an infant, washed and stroked and cared for. And then her scalp began to sting as though beset with swarming bees, and her eyes watered from the fumes, and she was engulfed by invisible kerosene clouds.

The next spring, on a March afternoon of rain-spitting wind, Thomas was napping in the big wooden drawer she'd lined with blankets. She was chopping onions and sniffling over them. She hurried to finish before Thomas woke.

John came in and put the kettle on. It wasn't his habit to make his own tea, and she looked up to see what the trouble was.

"I'm going to the bend tonight," he said. She put the knife down and folded her hands. "There's more work in the city."

"It's too dangerous to ride the rails."

"Supplies are running low," he said. She nodded, thinking of the root cellar showing patches of dirt floor. "It's for the baby."

"The baby needs his father. If you get caught … or fall—" She covered her eyes.

"I know what I'm doing." He warmed his hands around the kettle. "Don't you think I know what I'm doing?"

Thomas began to shriek as the kettle whistled. She wiped her hands on her apron and reached for him, unbuttoning her blouse.

"John," she said, staring at the steam rising as he poured.

"I'm going tonight. You'll be happy enough to see some money."

She wished to argue but knew he meant to have the last word. And there was no disputing the hard times. She pictured the Depression—that's what they were calling it—as an enormous pit in the earth. They were ants crawling at the bottom, working all day for their little crumbs. It surely must be different in the city. She thought of Jackson and his well-fed family out for a stroll in the park. They wouldn't be struggling. Perhaps they'd had to let some hired help go, but that would be the extent of it.

That evening they sat in the kitchen, pretending to read as the clock ticked on toward the 11:15 freight train that rattled their windows every night. She opened the Bible and flipped the pages a little too hard, so that one of them tore at the edge. He looked up.

"What about the tramps?" she said. "I don't mind giving them a bit of food when they come around, but you never know how they'll take it." She couldn't bear the thought of him riding the countryside like a tramp, aimlessly searching. It hurt her to think of that train carrying him away. She wanted to give him a morsel of nourishment, some salve for his wounds. But she couldn't say these things.

"I'll be home as soon as I can. Try not to worry." He smiled weakly. "I'll send the money back."

She flipped the pages back and forth.

Photos fell out of the back cover. Their wedding day, though you'd never know it from the plainness. There hadn't been time or money for finery. A picture of her parents, younger then, sternly posed. A group of youngsters on a hay wagon, baking in the sun. She traced her finger across the faces, first her own, then John in the second row at the end, Ivy next to him smiling coyly at the cameraman, and then circling back to stop at Jackson. She stroked the spot.

John stood up and his chair fell over with a crash.

"I'm going now," he said to her straightened back. He waited for a minute, then muttered something she couldn't make out and left.

How long did she sit there, eyes pointed at the picture but not seeing? Afterward, she went to bed, but sleep wouldn't come in that drafty house. She saw John heading out back to the trail, finding his way to the rail line, and then, crouched low at the bend, waiting for his chance. Over and over he missed the open car and fell under thundering wheels, screaming. What would become of them?

And when he finally crept back into bed, before dawn, she didn't turn to him, because she had won. Whether he changed his mind or lost his nerve or no longer trusted her to stay at home, didn't matter. She exulted in his return, cold righteousness in her mouth. She was too young to know that he'd blame her for his lost opportunities. For believing in the picture instead of her man.

"My father was fit to bust about his building."

Kathleen startled at the voice and opened her eyes. Jackson stood by the window, looking out over the flower gardens softly lit by the first golden streaks of daybreak. He ran the flat of his hand across the glass, stopping to press on it several times as if checking for flaws.

"He always had to have the best of everything, the finest workmanship, richest materials. His building was a statement that the Newsoms had arrived, you see. As much a statement as a headline in a newspaper, only brickwork and glass. It took up a whole city block."

She pushed herself up by the elbows to nearly seated. He had never told her much about his family or their business matters. Ivy liked to mention the Newsom Merchant Bank and Newsom Assurance as if they were cousins alongside Jackson. Kathleen had no idea what assurance was, and she'd be damned if she would ask.

"I started to do this trick, first for the employees, and then he'd make me do it for visitors." Jackson moved back from the window and ran toward it, pushing off the wall with his foot at the last moment. He turned toward Kathleen. "I could charge the window and rebound without breaking the glass. I just bounced off."

Jackson reached into his pocket for rolling papers and pouch tobacco. He sat on her bed and began to roll a cigarette on his thigh, brown crumbs falling onto the coverlet.

"Want one?" He held the cigarette toward her.

Kathleen frowned. "You still smoke?" She wagged her finger at him playfully, clicking her tongue.

Jackson lit a match on the bottom of his shoe and touched it to the end of the cigarette, cupping his hand like he was outside. He inhaled, held the smoke in, and watched her with narrowed eyes.

"So you ran straight into the window?" she said. He blew perfect smoke rings in the air above her head.

"All the time. It showed what stern stuff my father's building was made of." Jackson chuckled mirthlessly. "We lost a lot of money in the Crash, and after. People needed a laugh. I didn't see any harm in it." He shrugged his shoulders and settled back into the chair. "There you have it. The full account."

Kathleen shook her head. The smoke was fogging her in.

"An accident. Not what you wanted at all. But how did …?"

"The newspapers liked to write up my family. Any whiff of scandal and those hounds were on it. Of course, it was all between the lines back then. Now—hell, now they'd have blood-spatter patterns and witness statements. Grief counsellors for the staff."

"You know what they'd do now?" she said. She felt a tight pain in her forehead and rubbed the spot.

He grinned. Sticking the cigarette in his mouth, he reached over to plump her pillow and let a hand rest on her forearm. "The article said that I fell, and that's all it took for everyone to think it was money troubles that drove me to it. Not a single person in the room that day told them it was just a silly boy's game gone wrong. A mistake."

Kathleen patted his hand. It was cool and smooth, no calluses. He had been a silly boy; she should have seen that more clearly. John was dependable.

"They were afraid of looking foolish. And my father—" Jackson stopped to clear his throat. "My father preferred to let on that I'd jumped. I guess it gave me an air of gravity. He always wished I would be more serious."

"Gravity," Kathleen said, laughing as Jackson mimed a bird hitting the ground. She pushed at the outer corners of her eyes to staunch them.

"He never talked to the press; that was a strict policy. But he kept sending them reports about our financial recovery, and in two weeks, they forgot about me. The company did well."

"And your mother?" Kathleen said.

"She thought the worst, like you did."

Every part of Kathleen's body ached in the morning. She made snow angels in the sheets; it helped some to move around. The early light through the blinds reminded her of butter under a pastry blender in her hand. And waking on the farm in summer as a girl, the day spread out and already known: chickens to feed and water, the weeding and the laundering, berries to pick. The rhythm of chores and smells and sounds always the same. Until that summer when Jackson came to stay with his people who lived down the road, and the unknown washed over the known.

Her feet and fingers trembled from the waiting she had endured. She'd been living alone for years, brooding over events that could have been. Not paying enough attention to the life she'd had. She couldn't say exactly how long it had been going on, but enough was enough. Of that she was certain. She sniffed the air for smoke and brushed the covers in search of tobacco, but there was nothing to substantiate the conversation in the night, no lingering signs.

No matter.

Slowly, she reached for a bedpost to steady herself and threw off the covers, swinging her legs down, waiting for the buzzing in her head to stop. The floorboards under her bare feet were not as cold as she'd feared. It felt good to grip the smooth grain of the wood with her toes, like caressing her house. Any lingering lightheadedness would pass, she was certain, with fresh air. This was no day for her walker, or her clunky orthopedic shoes. She would get where she was going without the ugly aids that marked her as elderly. She'd be fine, shifting from one hand-fall to the next in the place where she knew them all. Moving this way reminded her of how Thomas had learned to walk, pulling himself to standing and then cruising between the sofa, radio console, and easy chair.

Her dressing gown hung on the back of the door. She reached for it, feeling the puckered seersucker fabric, and eased one arm in, and then the other. Her slippers were tucked behind the door. They slid on easily.

From the back porch, she side-stepped down the few stairs, holding the railing, and into the grass. Here the footing was trickier, but she kept the trail in sight, focussing on reaching it. Her breath was audible in her ears, yet she, who had been known for fretting over vexations large and small, did not stop to wonder if her pulse was racing too fast, or worry about looking ridiculous, should a neighbour happen to see her shuffling into the woods in her pajamas and robe. She spared no thought for anyone but Thomas, who planned to stop in this evening on his way home from work. Or was it tomorrow evening? Which day was this? She did love him so, her good boy. Still and all. The orderly passage of time might slip away from her, but the anchor of love remained. She should have told him more often how dear he was, how proud she was of him. And yet, she wasn't raised to voice such feelings.

Ahead, the sun broke above the trees, bathing the trail in the light of a new day that promised no harm. She turned back to glance at the house one last time before pressing onward. The opening to the trail, the spruce grove, the right turn onto the intersecting path, uphill to the ridge where the train slowed, at the bend. If she walked without ceasing, she would be there in time. The sun warmed her shoulders. Her joints felt limber and luxurious, fuelling her motion in a manner that belonged to an era she could barely recall. Her pace stepped up to match her quickening spirit.

The passenger express roared by every morning. Something told her Jackson would be on the train today, and John too. This time she wouldn't miss her chance. She'd leap through cloudless sky to reach them, grabbing their outstretched hands. She'd sit between them and tell the truth, a faithful rendering of herself. The scenery rolling by their window would make a pleasant diversion. She'd fill their ears with understanding as they rode along together.

Woman Cubed

The spells began as Dale was preparing for her break-through performance and also worrying about running into that man. For almost a year he'd been surprising her with pretty trifles left at the door—French soaps in the form of shooting stars; Belgian chocolate trapeze artists swinging across an edible tableau; a German doll that danced with a few turns of the key in her back. Each time, the neighbours claimed not to have seen a stranger in the building. As the company's prima contortionist, she was accustomed to receiving flowers, of course—on average, half-a-dozen men ordered roses in the afterglow of her intimate, impossible shows, each thinking himself a romantic genius—but the rabid fan sent African violets, one pot at a time.

Each delivery claimed space on the windowsill and added colour to the tiny white apartment, where nothing had lived with Dale and Derek before now. The plants reminded her of her mother. A woman ahead of her time in recognizing the spiritual benefits of connecting one's life force with the planet's flora, she had filled Dale's childhood with greenery, mostly big-leaf tropicals, light-hogs vying for the windows. As a young girl, Dale observed the outside world through perpetually dewy glass; it was like growing up inside a terrarium. Cradling an offering of *Saintpaulia inconspicua,* she inhaled the smell of dank earth, closed her eyes, and listened hard. When she heard the calm, ruthless snip-snipping of her mother's diminutive pruning shears, she was transported to a home that no longer existed.

She had been told two nights ago that recruiters from the Cirque—*that* Cirque, top of the top—would be coming to watch her. Insiders, people who no longer took calls from Derek but still liked her, whispered the news in her ear while she sat for dress-rehearsal makeup. She turned her head in surprise, and the bustling stage set tilted. Sound crews, spotlights, ropes slung in braids, and the costume lady pushing her rack of clothes all slipped sideways. Dale's vision cleared almost immediately, but her nervous system had been whirring and beeping ever since.

Derek made soothing teas and drew bubble baths, but she refused to relax. There was so much to do. It wasn't enough that she could fold herself like origami and squeeze into a clear acrylic cube not much bigger than carry-on luggage. She couldn't rely on her storied ability to dislocate shoulders and hips at will. A snake unhinges its jaw in order to consume larger prey, but that makes it a novel freak, not a blockbuster attraction. No, she needed to rebuild her act completely, starting with the brand.

She ran through new stage names as if testing ring tones. "Clarissa LaRose," the persona she'd adopted when Derek discovered her as a teenaged gymnast, was so over.

"Mi-mi-mi Mirandella, Mirella," she sang, trilling her r's. She stood on one foot and pulled the other over her head. In her flesh-coloured unitard, she was a living anatomy lesson. Not one

centimetre of her body was soft, yet she had the gift of making
bones dissolve. Her malleability passed for softness.

"La-la-la Lacrimosa, Milagrosa—no, that sounds fat."

Derek scribbled on a notepad. His greying shoulder-length
curls bobbed as he jiggled his crossed leg. "What's wrong with
the status quo?" he said. "Ditch 'Clarissa' and you've got zero
name recognition. I'm fond of Clarissa."

"Just fond? Not *in love* with?" She shook her ponytail at him,
which caused the room to wobble. When she dropped her foot
everything settled, but it felt temporary. Could the problem be
the azure-tinted contacts she'd just purchased? She was tired
of plain brown eyes and much preferred the startling intensity
of her new irises. "This is the last possible moment to change.
Once I'm in the big leagues, it's too late. Sorpresa, Spiritessa," she
said, "La Vida, La Viva, La Veda—"

"Dale," Derek murmured. He moved behind her, rubbing her
shoulders.

"What?" She leaned into his teddy-bear torso and tipped her
head back, then wished she hadn't. She gripped his arms around
her waist until the dizziness passed.

"*Dale*. What about Dale?"

"Totally inappropriate." She stepped clear of him. "Even you
can see that." She didn't mean to snap—so unlike the early days,
when she was Derek's adoring puppet-in-a-box. But what a pain
he'd been lately, arguing about every clause in her contracts,
alienating executives who only wanted more of her. He said,
"I'm protecting your interests," as if the company was some kind
of enemy. "Trust me," he always said.

He pointed both index fingers at her, thumbs up, like Old
West pistols. "It's the name your mother gave you. I'm just
saying."

She touched the vial that dangled from her necklace, a talis-
man worn at all times except during shows, when the relic ashes

of her mother posed a lethal hazard. She strived for a case-closed tone. "Mama understands that I have to change my name. An artist knows, in here," she said, tapping her chest.

"Oh, artists. The artists I've dealt with." Hands up, he retreated to the kitchen, calling, "Okay, you win. You and Mama Grow-op."

"Please. Like your mother can be tolerated for a single hour." She moved to the window and began to water each pot, taking her time, ignoring the clinking of dishes that Derek was washing extra-loudly.

"Let's not start that again," he said, appearing in the doorway, as she knew he would. "My mom didn't mean to insult you by bringing her own dinner—"

"I just think you should count your blessings. Lots of men would appreciate a dead mother-in-law." She lingered over the final pot, stroking the velvet tongue-like leaves, which would soon periscope a central cluster of purple buds on wavering pink stalks.

"If only she'd stay out of our creative decisions." She could sense, without turning to look, that he was smirking.

Unlike Mama, she wouldn't vent her rage with periodic bouts of wild slicing at the poor plants. If ever these violets grew large enough to be unruly, she'd confine herself to the calm and precise mode of pruning, cutting extraneous foliage for the plant's own good.

Derek cleared his throat. "Something else. Your friend. Again."

"My number one fan?" She straightened quickly, and then, regretting her haste, clutched her neck.

"I've informed the cops and, once more, they do nothing."

He punctuated the statement with an angry hand-clap, which reminded her of another time when he'd stomped his foot like a toddler. They'd had this argument before. The self-righteous expression on his face made her want to tip the spout of the watering can down the back of his shirt, but she kept the tone of her objection mild: "Is devotion such a crime?"

It wasn't as though she were oblivious to the myriad dangers posed by a strange man stalking her, but she preferred to view the situation from multiple angles, such as generosity and open-heartedness and unity and intrigue. Foreign concepts to the formerly charming Derek. Perhaps the guy was a little too into her—she could understand that as one possibility. But rather than a material being, a threat, wasn't he more like a wisp of smoke that wafted into their lives to warm them with memories of candles long extinguished? Who was to say he wasn't a messenger from the past, or the future? His coming might be the kiss of fate that revived her career.

When the notes first started coming, Derek reported a crazed stalker to the authorities, and they, in return, proposed a sting. Law enforcement would catch the guy in the act, some act of adoration. That was their plan.

"If you people think that I'd allow my wife, a performer of the highest calibre who will soon be famous worldwide, to be used as bait—forget it," he had said. "What happened to old-fashioned police work? Ever hear of that?" He threw the phone on the floor.

Dale had been stretching, preparing to enter her practice cube. She jackknifed into a fluid pike-press headstand. At times like this, Derek made more sense upside-down. "Do you think it's wise," she said, bicycling her legs, "to hang up on the cops? They also know where we live."

Now, spread out on the floor again, she wished she could just rehearse. The cube was in the corner of the bedroom, empty and gleaming. Calling her to come inside and disappear. Sometimes she had the sensation of splitting into facets: the single-jointed woman whose body took up the usual amount of space; the compressed woman imprinting the cube with her skin cells; and the spirit-woman floating above the spectacle, formless and free, able to see what the audience sees and report back. All three simultaneously. Not always, but at the best, highest moments of her art, it happened.

"What did he say this time?" She pushed her spine into the floorboards, one hand holding the vial of her mother's essence, dangling from its chain. She felt a warming glow spreading over her torso, and then the faint beat that synced with her pulse, racing and slowing according to her need.

"Same old," he said, hovering in the doorway with an apron tied around his middle, dust cloth in hand.

"Read it." She visualized the performance necessary to win over the Cirque: transcendent, personal best. Her special fan would be in the stands, boosting her chances. And Mama, admittedly not perfect, but motherish in the way she'd always been in life. Pushy and mouthy and indisputably on Dale's side.

"Nope. No way. I'm not going to read it."

"Read, Derek." Triumphant: her star discovered again, but bigger. "Darling."

"I've thrown it away. It's gone." He waved his hand in the air and left. She could hear him in the living room, rattling pots as he dusted around them.

"Careful with my violets! Come on, you keep ten-year-old gas receipts."

Derek draped the cloth over his shoulder and pulled a page of cream vellum from his pocket. Walking in again, he unfolded it, sighing. "'I offer the answers you seek.'"

"Hmm. And?"

"Your latest problem is a sign, he says. Sign of what, exactly? Such crap."

"What else?"

"Undying love." Derek reddened, as his volume rose. "The mystery man confesses love, how original."

She brightened. "See, some people appreciate artists. Give it," she said, holding out her hand.

"No, I don't think—"

"But I want it."

"What's the attraction here? You have trainers. You have a manager, me."

"Don't forget husband," Dale said.

"Funny. Stay away from this guy—I mean it." He walked a circle around her prone form, staring down in a way that was, she assumed, meant to intimidate.

"It's not like I'm meeting him secretly. I don't even know who he is." Her words turned cartwheels around her cranium, rapid revolutions of light, and then leeched from her nose to form a cloud of cotton candy suspended above her. She reached for a tuft, intending to taste it, when the whirling caught her again.

"Freaking nutcase," Derek said, dusting their dresser. "He shows up here, I'm throwing him down the stairs."

She puffed her cheeks, panting. "Never mind. What's *wrong* with me?"

Hours later, she lay in bed, fighting nausea, as Derek phoned the company doctor, physiotherapist, chiropractor, and psychic in turn. How unfair: her big moment finally here, and she couldn't imagine slithering through a tight maze of pipe, making crowds gasp, or hanging by her hair from a chain as children screamed. All she could do was stay still, suffering the bed spins of a common drunk.

Without examining her, the doctor diagnosed benign paroxysmal positional vertigo. "There's nothing benign about it," she said to the ceiling. Paroxysmal was a mystery, but positional she understood. Who knew positions better? And vertigo—a balance disorder, causes murky. No one could explain why nerve-dwelling crystals of the inner ear would suddenly migrate into the semicircular canals, leaving Dale reeling as they fled their ancestral homeland. Derek sat by her bedside and briefed her on uncertain cures: drugs, acupuncture, spinal adjustments, yogic manipulations of the head, and more.

"The doctor called in a prescription. You'll be normal in no time."

"Will that work? What did the psychic say? The show's the day after tomorrow." She paused, then yelled, "I should be practising."

"The truth? You're not performing. It pains me—a huge opportunity, don't think I don't know what this means to you—to us. But." He patted the quilt around her. "I'll speak to the honchos-that-be about getting another audition. I've still got connections at the Cirque. I can make that happen."

She moaned. "There has to be something else. Herbs, homeowhatever." She reached for his hand, gripping it. "Go. Out. And. Find. Me. Something."

"Darling—"

"Now!"

Dale drifted into thin sleep, recalling everything the fan had ever written to her. At first she found it creepy that he knew so much, like future performances that hadn't been announced yet. But the gifts piled up, no harm done. Over time, the guy began to seem *benign*. Like a super-active guardian angel. When she made some small change to her act, she found herself waiting for his reaction. He always noticed; his letters critiqued every new move.

Once he wrote, 'Stagecraft is a calling to destroy limitations. Hold your position five beats longer than you think you can. Subject the audience to your will. Release them with reluctance.'

"Hocus-pocus," Derek had said, adding that note to his collection.

At the time, she was coiled in her own limbs. Her voice began to waver as she entered the floating stage of practice. "I did try that one thing he suggested, craning my neck a degree counter-intuitively, and you know what?" She beamed in Derek's direction. "It worked." She moved through the splits before entering the cube.

"Dale? Don't listen to him. Hear me?"

She had stared through the clear wall, nose smushed, lips distended.

At dusk, still in bed and waiting for Derek to return with the treatments, her mother blew into her head. Since Mama's death, these fleeting appearances gave Dale a chance to ask questions, such as, Why the blah name? Were you depressed when I was born? What did you imagine my future would be? She wondered if she was living up to maternal expectations. Specifically, whether Mama was pleased with contortions as a line of work, and what she thought of Derek. Mama might appreciate Derek's nurturing side, but she was also quick to see a man's faults and prescribe harsh correctives, much as she might tackle an aphid infestation. Vertiginous, immobile, she heard Mama's pronouncements all too clearly: he's too old for you, his best days in the business are behind him, and he's no joy to look at—move on. "After the big show," Dale promised, half asleep. "Soon."

She woke not knowing the day or time. The doorbell had rung, she remembered. She thought that the physio who made house calls must have let himself in, but the man standing before her—tall, forbidding, angular—was a stranger. He took off his black fedora. His eyes fixed her in a cat-like green beam—real or contacts? She smiled, dazed. When he spoke, she heard bubbles in liquid. He might have said, "Your mother sent me." She hoped so.

The man helped Dale into her favourite position. He rolled her over so she was face down, then coached her into a backfold: legs curled up and over the head, feet planted in front of ears; pelvis stacked on head; chin in hands. Her abdominal muscles pulled taut, grounding her. She was a spider on the web, contemplative and wise. She could stay like this forever.

Heavy footsteps trudged up the stairs. Derek flung the door open. His voice barely reached her.

"I've got your medicine," he called from the hallway. He entered the bedroom and stopped. "What the—? Who's he—?"

The man, ignoring Derek, crouched to whisper in Dale's ear. He showed her a sprinkling of lavender pills, tiny pellets in his palm. "Extract of saintpaulia and other necessaries. Highly potent ingredients," he said.

She didn't move; she was stable and relaxed.

Derek rattled a paper bag. "*This* is your prescription. I've got it here."

The man stood and stared at Derek, who retreated to the hallway.

"Snap out of it, Dale. Don't take anything from him." Derek's voice receded to a muted echo of distortion, a meaningless buzz not without comfort.

The man stroked her throat. "Now," he said. She opened her mouth. He fed her the pills and closed her jaw. "Good girl."

"You were nothing before I found you," Derek shouted from somewhere in the apartment, his speech dagger-sharp again. "Your mother raised plants, and dick-all for you; *I* was the one who honed your talent."

The man gently helped Dale untangle and walked her to the cube. He held her hand as she slid inside.

"It's over," Derek yelled. A clay pot smashing reminded her of the tinkling piano interlude that accompanied the part of her act known as 'the dance of three impossibilities.' "You're finished. Who ever heard of a dizzy contortionist?"

Dale moulded herself to the cube's surface, angling her head downward. She felt fine. No spins, no spells.

Another pot crashed, then silence.

"Float on the surface of skewed perception," the man said. "Don't succumb to distraction's undertow."

Peace. Dale was the space available, no more, no less. The strictures of the cube fit perfectly.

"Give the performance of your life," the man said, tracing her face lovingly. He put his hat on and walked to the door, then turned back. "One more thing. From now on, you are La Reine Anguille."

"Queen Something," Dale said, or tried to say—her lips were stuck to the cube, yet he heard.

"Eel." The man tipped his brim and walked out, leaving her alone.

"Yes, La Reine Anguille," she breathed. "Just right."

Mother Makeover

Elaine watched Trevor Coleman watching his oversized TV on mute. He sat on his leather couch, a half-moon that anchored his company's prime office space, nearly penthouse. The widescreen monitor cast flickering light into the room, which Trevor kept in perpetual dusk with sleek taupe blinds that moved at the push of a button, sealing the windows. Walls papered in grasscloth and thickly carpeted floors added to an atmosphere unusually hushed for New York. When Elaine first arrived six months ago, she felt she'd stepped into a jewellery box. Her second thought was that no one would hear her if she screamed.

She fixed coffee the way he liked it, black with sweetener, and he didn't change position. He sat, legs sprawled, jaw locked. Not for the first time, she admired his ability to ignore everything but the current project. Focus, that's what set Trevor apart from the rest of the jackals in reality TV. He told her most producers lacked discipline. Sometimes they got far enough to secure financing, attach a name director or star, maybe make a pilot, but more often they went hungry, while Trevor's shows got made.

The monitor displayed a line of women on a sidewalk: standing, but not still. They paced, switched bags shoulder to shoulder, tilted hips, set arms akimbo, and raised them in mock supplication as the morning wore on. Many communed with phones, angling screens in the bright light as if sending signals with mirrors.

Viewed from the kitchenette where she was plunging the French press coffeemaker with practised control, the image seemed blurry, but when she blinked, individuals emerged. Every permutation of fat and thin, rich and not-rich, gay and straight; every race and age and fashion preference represented. A city of women, all talking. Even with the sound turned off, the buzz was obvious. Having a great time out there. How nice for them. Fuck crying, she wouldn't.

Why so emotional, Hillmer? In her head she mimicked Trevor's line about her supposedly flat-line affect, the level deadpan she deployed with him. He took it as a personal challenge to pry feelings from her. Which didn't mean she didn't have them. *You going to miss me, is that it?* The correct answer was *no*. She couldn't admit to sadness over the internship's ending next week. On the appointed day she'd simply disappear, no sodden farewells.

Across the room, the televised women mingled and snapped selfies. They wore numbered Coleman Productions badges. If she didn't know better, she would have guessed rally, or parade. It *was* parade weather: floral May breeze, flags snapping overhead. By August the breeze would die, leaving garbage and dog shit in every nostril, the flags limp rags, but today—they couldn't have ordered better conditions for an outdoor shoot.

At first she was lost, but when the camera panned the street, decorative grillwork covering lower windows on brownstones helped her identify the setting as the West Village, not far from the tiny walk-up she shared with three other film-school students. She searched the street for her parting gift, the big reveal minutes away. How Trevor would take it was an unscripted moment about to happen.

She approached the couch and waited while Trevor raised the remote control. The din was immediate: yakking New Yorkers accompanied by car horns, a fitting soundtrack. He set the remote on the massive glass coffee table, aligning it with a wireless microphone. She flattened his hand, wrapped his fingers around the mug, and squeezed before allowing him to support his own drink. Then, in the same mindful way her massage therapist maintained continuous contact, her hands leapfrogged from wrist to elbow to shoulder before landing briefly on his neck.

"How's it going?" she whispered.

Trevor grunted. Slurping from the mug, wincing at the heat, he remained fixed on the screen.

She sat beside him and drummed her knees. Where was her surprise gift? Allowing Rachel this platform had seemed like a good idea, but tension ticked at the base of her skull. If she could escape this scene, if she could will her spirit to flee, leaving behind an empty body to keep him company on the couch, she'd do it.

The TV registered a hubbub as Manuel appeared. She stretched her neck, dropping first one ear to shoulder, then the other. None of the contestants could match Manuel's looks—tall and thin, wearing low-rise jeans and a clingy shirt that dropped smoothly into the waistband. A wire headset crossed his clipped white-blond hair; he carried a microphone, and a bullhorn dangled from a strap around his other wrist. She brightened when the camera lingered over Manuel's cowboy boots and surveyed nearby shoes for context. His footwear was ironic, of course, but what did that mean in a women's reality show? Her hunch was that shoes could make or break it. He stepped his magnificent boots this way and that. Women followed, roiling the lineup.

Trevor grunted again, but at what? Manuel flashed a generalized smile of perfectly white, capped teeth, and everyone smiled back.

She had become accustomed to dealing with lower-echelon celebrities like Manuel Santiago. Having recently lost his gig interviewing owners of outlandish pets, he was available, and Trevor picked him up freelance. When she handed him the revised contract yesterday, he said, "So what did he do to me this time?" flipping pages to check Trevor's strikethroughs. Then he found her note alerting him to Rachel's presence and said, "Fine, I'll take care of her. See you later—well, you'll see *me*."

"And our contestants," she said.

"Yes, the mothers. Honour thy fabulous mother."

"Right?"

As Manuel worked the crowd, everyone swivelled, orienting to his magnetism. Elaine visualized a caption: the beauty/power equation. Trevor, too, attracted admirers with his ever-tan skin, shaved head, and impeccable suits, but it didn't translate on-camera. You had to feel it in person.

"Wow, incredible," she said, noticing Manuel's nipples clearly defined under his t-shirt, even the ring piercing the aureole of one nipple.

Trevor raised a hand. She wished she could retract the wow.

He leaned forward and spoke into the mic. "May twelfth. CP open call. Our newest and best reality project. At the end of the day, fifty gals will audition, out of the hundreds, no, thousands, waiting to dazzle America. Some spent the night on the sidewalk—that's how committed they are." He smirked. "Begin at the beginning, Manuel. Ask these ladies who they are."

Manuel pressed his earpiece. The camera zoomed in on his hesitation.

"Manny looks like he misses whacked pets, Hillmer." Trevor flicked her knee. "I expected more presence from him."

She reached for his mug. If only he would call her by her first name, and maybe look at her. He was a casual toucher from the beginning, which startled her at first, but she'd accepted that in her boss and now touched back as if they were affectionate old friends, and this was totally normal.

She doubted that Trevor could describe her. He didn't seem to notice her toned legs or short, flippy skirts. He probably had no idea that she really needed her giant black-framed glasses to read his endless lists. He never commented on photos tacked to her bulletin board, shots of her roommates on the High Line and her parents back in Virginia. Down the hall he kept platoons of staffers, but just the two of them occupied his personal office, and one was invisible.

Trevor spoke into the mic. "Ask the worst thing they've done, something they've never told anyone."

She refilled the mug and again sat next to him. She wouldn't admit to her roommates that she served coffee. They'd scored placements with indie filmmakers; reality TV didn't exist for them. But Trevor was a big name; she'd pay to be his audience. When he asked her opinion, she forgave him for things he hadn't even done yet.

"So you think," she said, to cover her shakiness, "the 'most horrible thing' will come out in some random interview? A stranger with a microphone, and they're spilling dirt?"

"Wait for it."

Manuel worked the line with his reporter face—open, ready to be amazed, instant best friend.

"He's got presence," she said. "Those old ladies, they're eating him up." She searched for a particular old lady.

"Stop it, Hillmer. Manny doesn't go for girls, you know." Trevor cleared his throat. "Maybe you didn't know."

Onscreen, Julie from Long Island: "I got so drunk I didn't hear my toddler. She's swimming in her own vomit, *literally swimming* in her bed, and I—" she grimaced. "'Mommy, mommy,' but no one came!" Julie mopped mascara streaks.

Julie's teenaged daughter reached for the mic. "It's okay," she cooed. "See? No scars. I love you, Mom."

"One night of drinking, who cares?" Trevor said.

Manuel moved on.

"The worst? Food stamps. Rough times, right?" said Halina, bird-like in filmy layers of dancewear. "My kids ate nothing but hot dogs for years. It was a form of child abuse, I admit it."

"And?"

"And today we eat organic." Halina chewed her fingernail. "A hundred miles."

Trevor punched the cushion. "I'm sleeping here."

Maureen's exaggerating lips filled the screen. "We—you know, *did it*, while the kids were in our bedroom."

"I'd sleep with her," Trevor said, cocking an eyebrow at Elaine. "I would. What about you?"

"Ahh …"

"Any regrets?" Manuel said.

"Regret is a waste. You only go around once, right?" Maureen laughed heartily.

Her daughter, spiky-haired and pierced, stepped in front, scowling. "That's not what you tell me."

Trevor pointed. "She might be okay—energy between the characters, at least. Flag her."

Elaine went to her desk. As she reached for her clipboard, she pressed her forehead into the fibre-covered wall as though burrowing. The comfort this scratching post provided mystified her, but it never failed. She marked Maureen's number.

Manuel moved more rapidly. "Quick, your worst!"

Standing behind Trevor, Elaine said, "What's the worst thing *your* mother ever did? Not that it's any of my business, but I wondered what inspired you to create this show."

The camera panned faces as Manuel repeated, "worst motherly move." He began using the bullhorn, sending his lengthened, deepened voiceover through the crowd. Women stepped forward one by one.

"Threw her out when she said, 'I hate you.' Hate your own mother!"

"Stole her boyfriend."

"Pressured her to be like her smarter, prettier older sister."

Trevor shrugged. "Money, what else?" He fell silent. "Worst to me? Or worst in general?"

"Is there so much to choose from?" Elaine almost sobbed but managed a speculative "Hmm." Poor Trevor. She should have hung up on Rachel.

A tanned bodybuilder in platform sandals and a mini-dress showcasing muscle pushed forward, saying, "Strict diet. She's out of control." She prodded her daughter, whose face reminded Elaine of oatmeal. A loose grey sweatsuit hid the girl's figure.

"Them," Trevor said, startling her.

"Why?"

"Beauty and the beast thing? Two different beasts."

Sweat trickled past Manuel's headset. The women jostled him. He chose a petite blonde in tennis whites, chewing gum. The handle of a racket protruded from her red, white, and blue tote bag. Her tennis bracelets sparkled when she smoothed her hair.

"Okay: How do you tell your kids you love them?" Manuel said. "Do you post Facebook status updates? Do you tweet your love?"

"Please, a mother's love is too big for Twitter. I need more space."

A blousy woman with a cloud of dark hair chimed in. "No, Manny-baby. You gotta love 'em where they live, and those kids live on their phones. Tweet, tweet, tweet is my advice."

"Who are you, Dr. Phyllis? Butt out." The tennis player snapped her gum. "Manuel, a lot of buttinskys came today. FYI, I'm the mom the American people will cheer for. And FYI again, I love your strange pet show so, so much!"

Manuel looked past both of them.

Trevor slumped. "Where are the insanely competitive stage mothers, the failed suicides, the junkie moms who'll relapse for our entertainment? Where are cigarette marks on innocent heinies? I want Momzilla, Manny."

"So what should I ask?"

"Ask them to brand themselves. Three words max. Be careful about the ones who've been to reality TV school—they'll have a dramatic persona ready. I want *real* real."

What brand of mother was Rachel? Tenacious. Needy. Calling over and over, but Trevor wouldn't take the calls. Rachel filled Elaine in—ten years estranged from her only son, not a word spoken. There was still no sighting. Elaine wasn't sure what Rachel looked like, but she'd recognize the voice instantly: New Jersey brash, gruff but also plaintive, wheedling.

Manuel turned circles, yelling into the bullhorn, "What KIND of mother are you? If you were a brand, what would it be? BLANK MOM, something Mom."

"Maybe our concept needs work." Trevor patted the cushion next to him.

She came around to sit, hugging her clipboard. "And the concept, *our* concept, is motherhood, but with an edge, right? The good and the bad. Reunions and real talk: *Motherhood, Apple Pie, and Dirt.*"

"Nah, I hate that. I changed it to *Mother Makeover.* So you get these horrific moms, each one a different problem. Something needs to change—"

"According to the kid?"

"Doesn't matter. Someone sees trouble. We get them experts. Issues, tissues, they walk out all—"

"Perfect."

"I don't know perfect, but better."

"Interventions—call it *Group Therapy*."

"That's been done. Also, it has to be heartwarming, an upward narrative arc to end each episode—like one of those angel shows or *The Waltons*."

"What's *The Waltons*?"

"Way to make me feel ancient, Hillmer. For real, you never saw it, even in syndication? You know"—Trevor switched to falsetto—"'Good night, John Boy,' good night whatever the other hicks were called." His voice returned to normal. "Heartwarming."

"Nope." She jotted notes. "It shouldn't be hard to find bad mothers. They're everywhere. There should be a test before people can procreate."

"Not *too* judgmental. How many kids you have?"

"Being a parent isn't required to recognize bad parenting. Ever been trapped on an airplane with a screaming brat? That's terrorism." She coughed. "You have kids?"

"Two."

"Really?"

"No, two hundred. Really."

"It's just …" She studied the walls, an unrelieved swath of savannah. "Pictures?"

"Long story, Hillmer. We're not close. Hey, I wonder if my ex-wife would go on the show. Now, *she* was a damaging mother." Trevor gestured at the screen. "Watch."

"Hippie Mom," said a young woman carrying a naked baby. She pried her dreadlock from the baby's fist. "Chill."

"Barbie Mom," said a model in a tiara and princess gown.

"Six-Pack Mom," said the bodybuilder, dragging her lumpen daughter. "No pain, no gain Mom."

"We've seen them already," Trevor said. "Fame whores."

"Rehab Mom," whispered a pale, skinny woman. "In recovery."

"Get her number," Trevor said, but Elaine had already recorded it.

Jewish, Italian, and Jewish-Italian moms; Born-Again, Perfectionist, Chef moms, and more paraded past, until Trevor interrupted; Manuel made a time-out sign.

"Okay, we've got some maybes," Trevor said. "Next, just saunter along, they saunter too. You'll come to a small cross street: turn right. Everyone follows Manuel, the Pied Piper of Santiago. And then it's game time."

She frowned, flipping through her copy of the treatment.

"You give three gals this message. Say *only the first twenty* to the studio will be *allowed* to audition."

"Not the ones—I thought fifty—you select?" she said.

Manuel turned his back to the camera and murmured, "Only twenty? How will that work?"

"I've got cameras hidden all along the route."

"You're the boss," Manuel said.

"I thought we were checking them in and taking their tapes," she said.

"All those tapes? No fucking way."

"What *are* we doing?"

"He tells three friends; they tell three friends." Trevor smiled for the first time that day. "Poof, viral."

"What is this, *The Amazing Race*?" Elaine said. "Speed is what counts? Not personality or backstory or looks?"

"Keep going, Manny." He lowered the mic. "Yeah, Hillmer, it's a race. They'll run, trip each other, pull hair and scratch, all live. It's going to make great TV."

"What if they can't run? What about the slower ones?"

He turned up his palms, letting the mic dangle between two fingers.

"Too bad for them? Is that it?" She saw by his irritated glance that he thought she was being shrill. She took a deep breath. "It doesn't seem fair is all, changing the rules halfway through."

"Sue me. They'll do what it takes to get on national television."

She refused to look at him. Her chin quivered.

"Okay, Hillmer, last lesson from the grizzled veteran." He gently touched her cheek. "Yes, I realize you'll be gone next week—I get that, see? You think you have to tell me everything." She ducked her head.

"So I thought, what if something interesting happens before the show starts? Not a whole series' worth, but an episode, maybe a couple weeks. It's a meta thing, frame around the frame, get it? Take the raw footage of audition day, ramp up the drama, add obstacles and whoa! A show about creating a show. Everything happens on the street, and they don't even know they're on the show yet."

She sat very still.

"Now *you* say, 'Brilliant.'"

Why offer ideas? She was getting a credit on this show, albeit a lowly intern credit, but had no idea what they were making.

"Speak."

She summoned images of Trevor in a nursing home of the future, dribbling coffee on his bib, sending her derivative pitches for stupid shows.

"I think it's been done."

"Truce?" He patted her thigh. "Friends."

She tried for a feisty response, but bleakness filled her. They weren't friends. She was a prop, easily replaced. After next week, she'd never touch him again. She couldn't say when that had become a mainstay for her. She guessed it had happened through repetition, the daily person-to-person contact becoming part of the package.

Onscreen, Manuel pulled a woman out of the crowd. She was tiny, wearing red sunglasses that gave her the aspect of an insect. Maroon curls escaped from a chiffon head-wrap. "Where's the camera?" she said and upon hearing that raspy, elated voice, Elaine bolted to standing.

"Jesus," Trevor said.

"So," Manuel said, putting his arm around the woman, "what kind of a mother are *you*?"

"Fuck!" Trevor brought the mic to his mouth and then lowered it.

Rachel turned her head side to side, projecting her voice to the wings of an imaginary stage. "Trevor, are you listening? It's Mommy."

Elaine thought her vertebrae might tumble like a child's tower of blocks. She knelt on the tabletop.

Trevor launched himself off the couch. "This isn't happening."

Rachel's onscreen face presented a female version of Trevor's angularity. A softer, more appealing version. Elaine wished she could glide across the glass and stroke Rachel's skin, so close and real, but not touchable.

"First of all, I forgive you for not calling on Mother's Day." Rachel paused, courting the masses. "What's Mother's Day, after all? Just a day like any other day. I know, I know. You're busy." Laughter rose around her.

Elaine studied the image of the person who went with the unignorable telephone voice. Girlish circles of blush couldn't hide her pallor. A close-up of her Gucci clutch revealed the bag as a knock-off, her fingernails jammed with dirt.

Trevor moved toward her. "You knew about this."

She half-shook her head, more a wish for denial than denial itself. He pulled her by the arm off the table. She dropped awkwardly onto carpeting as he stood over her.

"You arranged it."

"You're live."

Manuel looked confused; he held Rachel's shoulder as if he thought his interview subject might flee.

Trevor raised the mic to his lips. "Never mind. Finish up with this one as fast as you can—ditch her, hear me?"

"Isn't she your—"

"I said move on. She's nobody."

Rachel addressed Manuel. "Life!" She faced forward again. "Honey, I'm sorry to the moon. How much sorrier can I be?"

"Gee, I think I've heard this," Trevor said.

"Yeah, there's a time and place for our private info. But I have news for you: heart trouble. I take all these pills just to keep a steady beat."

"Since when does she have a heart?"

Elaine felt Trevor's weariness beneath his son schtick. He went to the window and reached out as if to move the blinds aside, and then reversed course, heading back to the couch, and the screen.

When Manuel tried to leave, Rachel wrapped herself around him. She let herself be a dead weight as he walked.

"Tentacle Mom," Elaine said, still kneeling on the floor.

"Yeah. Life-sucking, never-ending." Trevor loosened his tie. "Mother of all leeches."

"Why don't you talk to her?"

"Now you've really lost your mind."

"She's going to run to the finish line? What about her bad heart?"

"Did I invite her? I won't be manipulated."

Rachel continued talking over Manuel's shoulder. "Hey, Trevor," she yelled. Manuel stopped walking, and she slid off. "Maybe your goons—no offense, Manuel—don't believe I'm your mother. Here's a little story to prove it."

"Cut her off!" Trevor said. The crowd was rapt. Elaine crept to the couch and sat a body's width from Trevor.

Manuel took off his headset, pointing at Rachel.

"When Trevor was born he had a tooth, a tiny pearl in his precious mouth. And on your right foot, Trevor, an extra toe—you had six! Two were fused together. Webbed like a duck. Right from the start, you were special."

Elaine couldn't help glancing at Trevor's hand-stitched brogues, just as he straightened his legs, thrusting them under the coffee table.

"Did I blame you for being different? An innocent babe nursing at my breast? Such a strong sucker, that one. Never let go."

Trevor flinched.

"Great footage," Elaine said.

"We'll edit this out."

"Of course I didn't blame him, who would? But!" Rachel raised a finger. "Let a mother screw up, say she's not the model of perfection, and then shit flies. Am I right?" She waved her arms. "Lemme hear you." Whoops came back, and stagey *Mmm hmmms*. "Show me a mother who makes mistakes and I'll show you the naming, shaming, blame game. Everyone blames mothers. Don't they?!" Cheers erupted. "The kid turns out bad, it's the mother's fault. He makes something of himself, becomes a big producer, say, with lots of money and everything money can buy ..." She lowered her voice. "Well, then, he's a self-made man. Did it all himself, in spite of his crazy mother."

Trevor looked bemused. "We might be able to use some of this."

"Trevor?" Rachel's audience fell into a respectful silence. "Trevor!"

She swayed, insubstantial beneath the chiffon crown. Manuel led her to the curb, where other women supported her on her way to the sidewalk. They fanned her as she pawed the air. "Do I get to be on the show?"

Manuel stared at his headset as if seeing it for the first time. Finally, he put it on.

Trevor spoke quietly. "Hey, thanks, pal. That was great. I owe you one."

Rachel's wails faded as Manuel retreated. He wiped his temple. "Just tell me what's next. Let's get this over with."

"We have to help your mother," Elaine said.

"Next the turn, and then the message: the ladies have to beat each other to the studio."

The women surged around Manuel. "Okay, okay," he said, circling. He began walking, and they fell in behind him.

"Good," Trevor said. "Almost there—turn right."

Manuel strutted, waving his followers behind him. He swivelled and marched backwards like a drum major, swinging the bullhorn in loops around his body. "Are you sure this is the place? It's an alley."

"Just do it."

"Okay, chief. Here we go—turning." Manuel spread his arms, making like an airplane. "Come on, ladies," he yelled, then remembered the bullhorn and brought it to his lips. "This way to the audition."

"Where does the alley lead?" Elaine scratched red streaks into her wrists.

Manuel found the bodybuilder and whispered into her ear. She nodded, pulling her daughter into a jog.

The girl dragged her feet, screaming, "No, Mom. No more running."

"Do you want to be a fat nobody for the rest of your life? Come *on*."

Manuel whispered to another woman, who told another. A few started running, then more.

Trevor rested his head on Elaine's shoulder. "So why didn't you invite *your* mother to audition, huh?"

"My mother? We don't have any issues."

"Live a few more years. You will."

The truth was she couldn't reconstruct a precise motivation in this Rachel business. There was the tug she felt when Rachel pleaded, *Give me a shot, hon, I just need a chance*—yet the same tired line from a would-be starlet wouldn't have moved her. There was the prospect of effecting change, as if she were a documentary filmmaker exposing a wound and letting the audience participate in its healing. Or maybe it was simpler, and closer to the heart: her last chance to do something Trevor would remember.

She said, "I just thought it would be good dramatic TV—the mother–son reconciliation." Elaine waited for him to explode.

"B+," he said. "I accept your apology."

"Are they going to a set? A studio, what?"

"It's a dead end."

"You're joking."

"Now, Manny, run as fast as you can; catch up to the front-runners. You can do it, big guy—they're wearing heels. About a quarter mile, you'll come to a yellow door on the left. Go through the door—just you—and you're done."

Manuel planted his boots, hands on hips. "I have to run? Seriously? That wasn't in the contract. And what about your mother? Don't you want me to bring her with?"

"New York fucking Marathon, you moron. Run!"

Manuel glowered and pushed off, pumping his arms, leading the way.

Elaine watched Trevor watching the women running and felt as cold as the November day she'd spent at the actual New York Marathon, cheering for a friend lost in the mass of runners. A slope in Central Park provided a decent view, but soon it made her nauseous to follow the conveyer belt spilling people down-hill. The same now: too many to track.

And these people weren't marathoners. They ran without pacing themselves, sprinting for an unknown finish line. Some held hands, bags bouncing between them. Elbows and knees and spike heels became weapons. There was no longer friendly noise, just grunts and pounding feet.

Elaine had never seen Trevor like this: he had a sweat going, a glow. He licked his lips; she pressed hers together. She hoped that Rachel was still on that curb, safely abandoned.

The women began to yell, some encouraging, others angry. The alleyway narrowed, and the shouting became more urgent, beyond words. She remembered a nature film on the great migration of the Serengeti, and the thought of marauding wildebeests made her yelp hysterically.

Trevor frowned, as good as a slap to her face.

"You have to pull the plug," she said. "It's too dangerous."

"How?" he said, without interest. He sounded distracted, but only if you were giving him the benefit of the doubt. And why should she? Why was her default position that he was benevolent, despite any supporting evidence? Accusation rose within her.

"Look how worked up they are. It's Black Friday at Wal—"

"Who knows why people do what they do? I'm not responsible for their choices. They want to be stars."

Some women cried out as they were pushed; others fell silently. The leaders reached the end of the alley, turned around, and met the force of the oncoming wave. There was no group identity anymore, just individuals scrambling, water molecules set to boiling.

"My God," she said. "What's going to happen to that one with the baby?"

She wanted to shake Trevor, make him listen, but she couldn't stop watching the screen long enough. She tried to find people: the bodybuilder's daughter, the dancer, the drinker. They seemed like missing friends. And Manuel, Rachel—nowhere.

The women kept coming, but there was no space. They fell and were fallen upon. The camera panned debris on the pavement—spilled handbags; a tiara; a platform shoe resting against a ballet flat.

Trevor's face was lit from within or maybe from the TV. He squeezed the bridge of his nose and whispered, "I didn't think this would—"

"You didn't mean to hurt anyone," Elaine prompted, reverting to the benevolence script. "That wasn't the plan." And immediately she interrogated herself: Was this gullibility? Self-protection because she had admired him and worked for his approval? She wanted to think of herself as generous, but willfully blind was a contender too.

"No, but that," he said, gesturing at the monitor as though acknowledging a performance worthy of applause.

Motion slowly died. Bodies filled the screen: dazed, moaning, crying, but people couldn't be linked with their sounds anymore. Elaine and Trevor watched from the protection of the couch's big curve, their feet, knees, hips, and shoulders fused. She was chilled, shattered, but pressed against him as if she still had valuable ideas to contribute, as if he weren't repulsive.

Until this moment, she hadn't realized that people could be physically close and psychologically alone. In her half-year with Trevor she'd concocted an intimate storyline for two creatives cut off from the world in their shuttered cave, but it could never happen that way. Here they were, practically a single panting organism, yet isolated from one another, alien and unknowable.

Sirens shrieked and multiplied, drowning out other sounds. The assault cycled on and off, starting up again just when it seemed as though silence would hold.

"Hillmer, get me Trish Coleman-Cohen on the phone."

"Okay," she said but didn't move. "Who's she?"

"My lawyer."

Mentally, she whipped across the room, the picture of auto-obedience, but in the physical realm, she couldn't force herself to leave the deceptive warmth of his body.

"And my sister."

A sister, of course. What more would be revealed? Were they done, already? Could she leave him now, have a life?

"She needs to know about this," Trevor said.

They sat tight, thinking unshared thoughts. Elaine followed the images on the screen as visual filler flooding her senses, nothing more, and certainly not a storyline she had any professional or personal investment in. She was too numb to worry about the fate of anyone inside or outside their hushed sanctum. Instead, she rehearsed the ways an aspiring filmmaker might choose to represent her concept of close isolation/isolated closeness. Film is good, film is great, but it conveys only so much. She considered using a fish-eye to simulate claustrophobia, zooming in to capture pensive expressions, pulling back for perspective, trying a two-shot, even a cheesy voiceover, but no sequence or combination would capture the meanings available in the scene they were living. Nothing she could imagine would expose the separate narratives of characters like Trevor and his intern, at cross-purposes with each other and possibly with themselves, their dialogue and actions, feelings and intentions always out of sync.

A Flock of Chickens

1. Cooped Up

Although there's a door of normal height, Rae-Ann enters the coop through a small square door cut into the back wall. She doesn't want to trigger the motion detector light, which her father installed so he could watch it flash on and off from the house and wait for predators lurking in the night, a situation that might require his shotgun. She enters the coop through the cavernous old shed where she once played hide-and-seek with her older sisters, diving behind dusty feed bins and garden equipment, trying not to give away her position with a giggle or a sneeze.

This was their fun as young girls, out in the country with no other kids around. Not for them the summer camps and organized sports that train children to elbow their way through life. Six years after leaving home for university, Rae-Ann still feels like a shocky transplant, set in the cold soil of Toronto without a hardening-off period. Daily, she braves the jammed streetcar that takes her to work; the boardwalk where speeding cyclists and rollerbladers force walkers to jump to the side; the beggars and buskers whose question-mark faces line her route home; and a bewildering array of decrees governing the disposal of her garbage. But none of it seems real. Real is memory: barefoot running on grass, ducking into the culvert as her sisters pound on the metal with stones, making it ring and ring. And now she's back, unexpectedly. How quickly she's escaped the troubling city.

From her old hiding place in the shed, Rae-Ann squeezes through the rough-framed opening and drags her body downward into the coop, scraping her sides. Her elbows take the brunt of her graceless landing on the plywood floor, which is covered with straw and droppings. She disturbs, is the disturbance raising fear. The shifting of creatures within stirs the air, an expectant fluttering. She senses cold eyes fixed on her, but nothing can be seen in the crowded darkness.

Rae-Ann's father pushes food and water through the little hatch-door in the winter, when snow blocks the outside access. Snow a natural insulator. He doesn't shovel if he doesn't have to. With a gloved hand he slides the feed tray and swings the water can expertly, tending his flock without wasting any time looking at them. What if one were to die, threatening the rest with disease? It never happens. Every spring they rush the open door, standing for a moment at the green threshold of life before hopping down to begin a fresh season of scratching.

The coop isn't winterized, but the birds don't freeze. Rae-Ann knows how it works: the feathers plump up, wrapping the body in a self-made quilt of air. She's taught it to her grade fives. Plumped feathers an involuntary response, like shivering in people. She digs her tiny flashlight out of her purse—acquired for urban emergencies, unused until now. The hens rouse themselves with soft chuckling and then fall silent, staring into the light. In her sweeping yellow beam, dust motes suspended in vapour, her breath made visible. Crap on the floor, a hilly topography of isolated brown and white lumps and piles rising like pyramids. An April wind blows in, lifting cobwebs from the exposed two-by-fours framing the coop.

Nine chickens roost on a pole, nestled together. Shared body heat another trick of survival. And the warmth generated by manure must help, although she feels no heat from the floor.

In her haste, Rae-Ann has underdressed for the weather and the dirt. Her flip-flops sink into half-desiccated muck. Wedged into the corner, she wishes for pinfeathers and companions pressing against her.

2. Chicken Feed

Last night in her empty apartment, Rick's voice echoed, robbing her of sleep. His lame joke while paying the cashier for their dinner earlier that evening, one of many fast-food meals they'd eaten together since she joined the small staff of Elmvale Road Public School in the fall. Rick had been teaching there for five years and made more money than she did as a first-year teacher, but he watched his spending. He always paid cash.

"Chicken feed," he announced to no one in particular. The cashier seemed to understand she was a backdrop to their conversation and didn't answer as she handed Rick his change. Or maybe she was just tired of customers who didn't tip. There was a jar next to the cash register, but it held only a few quarters. They looked for a table, balancing orange trays. "Cheap and cheerful," Rick continued in a hearty voice. "What's not to love about food like this?"

Rae-Ann had smiled, ever agreeable. But a different inter-
pretation came at night. His act was meant to show that nothing
was going on between them, co-workers eating under fluores-
cent lights in a public place, not touching. She wanted to touch
him for security, to feel his chest, his back. But he drove her
home right afterward. He wouldn't come in because he had an
early morning. As if she didn't.

Alone in her bed, she tried to see the relationship objectively.
There had been no fight, just a slow erosion of attention. When
they were away from school, it was worse. She had to entertain
him with animated stories, or else he fell silent and ate with great
concentration, stabbing his fries into little paper cups filled with
ketchup. He moved the cups around the tray, lined them up,
shot them into the corners. He crumpled his napkin and stood,
ready to slide the remains of his meal into the garbage before
she had finished eating.

They'd never said *love*. He wasn't her first; she could defer the
love conversation for a little longer. She could face, with reluctance, her growing need to dissect their "love"—its strained
quality, its asymmetry. But she hadn't anticipated the throwback
word, *cheap*. Cheap was idiotic, and yet it made her squirm. Her
value determined by arbitrary, external rules that society had
supposedly left behind—but the rules were still in play, imposed
by forces that overpowered her. Between shame and desire,
caught. She tried to lull herself with distractions. What to wear
the next day, what to say to her pupils. And that sparked fever-
ish lesson planning, one idea blurring into another, blotting out
Rick.

Who knows what it means to call something chicken feed?
One of them might get it, but it's unlikely—they're city kids
whose chicken comes in buckets, battered and fried.

In the coop, well after midnight, Rae-Ann rocks back and
forth, staving off cold. She taps her foot until it connects with

the metal tray and pushes it: empty. Even in her submerged state, she can gather facts. A clear intention forms. When the sun rises, she'll go into the shed and scoop feed for her new roommates. She'll let it run through her fingers, even taste it. Though she can't, just yet, imagine leaving this confined, sheltering space.

Chicken feed: a thing of no value, costing little. Synonyms: chicken scratch, chickenshit.

3. Home to Roost

Rae-Ann slides down the wall into a squat. She won't be able to hold this position. Soon she'll be sitting in the filth, stirring it with her feet just to keep busy. Chickens roost in the air, flying up for safety. At least she's not directly beneath them; the droppings won't hit her. And the stench no longer bothers her. At first, an acrid oppressiveness bore down, unbreathable. She gulped lungfuls of it to stay ahead of her body's need for oxygen. Now, with her quieter movements, the dust has settled. The air is perfumed with an undertone of sweet rot, unnoticed before; it seems more natural than the harsh ammonia overlay. The whole world is rotting, after all. She sinks into the odour as into a comforter, dozing on and off.

Not for long: her father will be coming. She was careful to park at the road and walk in, but eventually he'll see the car. And even if he doesn't, he'll come to collect the eggs and let the hens out before mid-morning, after he's read the paper and eaten his solitary breakfast. He'll want to know what she's doing here when she should be in the city, earning her publicly funded salary. Never mind what she's doing *here* here, brushing straw out of her hair, straining to see shapes in the dark.

She had been circling her apartment all afternoon, reviewing her losses, trying to think. She placed a call to her union rep. Swept floors, tidied up, watched the lights flicker on in buildings up and down the street. She doesn't remember a decision to drive north, or the trip itself, which normally takes three hours.

Her father will be disappointed, not surprised—he always expects the worst—by her disgrace. He'll stand outside the hatch-door, demanding facts. Confusion will make him less patient, not more. A vision: his large, craggy head turned sideways as he crouches down, bracing himself against the wood. His ear centred in the square. Her lips murmuring a confession: cluck-cluck cluuuuuck. Him backing away, unwilling to hear it.

In her poultry-themed lessons on language, all will be explained.

Boys and girls, when you play games instead of working, and you fail a test? The chickens have come home to roost.

4. The Pecking Order

Blades of light slice the sky when Rae-Ann's hunger asserts itself. When did she last eat? Dinner. Not this night that she has passed hiding in a ten-by-ten cell, but the day before, in the burger place.

Some of the hens have laid, getting a jump on the sun with long cackling litanies. She reaches into her purse for the penknife, given by her father so long ago, and flips it open. RAY is engraved on the handle, for Rae-Ann Yarrow, but also for Raymond Allan Yarrow, who carried the knife as a boy and later passed it on to her, never dreaming that it would cost him some of his harvest today. No matter. The flock is a hobby, not a living.

She stands up and stamps her feet. Ducking under the pole, she claps her hands at the hen in the closest nest box, a Barred Plymouth Rock. It's motionless.

"Shoo!" Rae-Ann waves the knife. It stands, not fast enough. She scoops it up and out—furious squawking and wing-beating, but a show. The egg is warm and covered with mucous. Rae-Ann wipes it. The knifepoint makes a neat hole. She raises the egg to her lips and sucks. It's slippery, neutral. She throws the shell into the corner.

A school day dawns. Who will teach her class? Dear students with awkward growth spurts and runny noses, unaware of the rough weather of puberty looming. The boys' dirty fingernails, the girls' highlighted hair—Rae-Ann is appalled by the many signs of parental idiocy on display in her classroom, yet she still loves her children; they are not at fault. Do they love her back? As much as Rae-Ann would like to believe she's a fixture in their lives, it's not hard to envision the supply teacher's campaign to win them over. Three days, and they'll forget about her.

What have they been told—that she's ill? She doesn't want to consider whether an illness grips her, something like her mother had years ago, before she died, when she needed a rest and disappeared into the hospital. Her father handed young Rae-Ann all the kitchen duties with none of the instructions. Her sisters cleaned, shopped, and did laundry. She knew how to cook only pancakes and eggs, so they ate that for a month, and no one complained.

When Rae-Ann began her first year of teaching, her new colleagues gushed advice and resources, but she held them off. She had never been able to embrace instant friends. Also, she was bad at pretending to admire their methods, which were at odds with her training. They used pre-fab worksheets and Disney movies. She showed them her portfolio fresh from Teacher's College. When Joyce suggested that she screen *Pocahontas* during the unit on Indigenous peoples, Rae-Ann thought she was kidding. She said, "Sure thing, and let's show *Mulan* for the unit on China." It took a beat for the tone to hit. Joyce inhaled sharply but kept her face a mask of professionalism.

Soon, she wished that she'd accepted help. Students chattered as she presented her sweat-offerings, lessons that often didn't end right. Her legs ached, and she felt shaky, like she was getting the flu. Parents wanted old math; to her astonishment, they wanted the worksheets. She was called into parent-teacher conferences with her principal, Sue, who liked to "build bridges," but each compromise hurt Rae-Ann. Sue should have backed her up. By January, none of the women teachers would share a cup of tea with Rae-Ann; the staffroom emptied soon after she arrived. They passed her in the halls with bright, empty smiles.

Only Rick kept her from quitting. He coached her through the behaviour problems—kids and parents—and informed her that Joyce was an alcoholic and Sue a control freak. Rae-Ann shouldn't waste time worrying about Joyce, but she could impress Sue with upbeat reports. One morning Rick left a vase of pink chrysanthemums on her desk, just because. They went out for a coffee that afternoon, and he snapped a photo of them on her phone. He came around the table to her side, leaning his head close as he took the picture, and then he stayed there.

At staff meetings, she sat beside him, flaunting their alliance, cheeks burning. They were jealous, the old hags. Rick was young and slender and strong, the only man on staff, their darling mascot. On yard duty at recess, he enticed the kids into raucous games of keep-away, which ended in a mass tackle and lots of happy screaming. "Come get the ball!" Holding it overhead, laughing. "Try to get it—come on!" He always let them catch him in the end, falling to the ground as they pulled at his clothes. Although there was a strict no-contact policy, the other teachers didn't object. All they ever did was gawp at him like smitten girls.

Frost covers the coop's sole window. Rae-Ann scrapes her

fingernail against the glass, trying to see over to the house. He'll be drinking his coffee now. The flock grows restive, scratching around the watering can skimmed with ice. There will be water when the temperature rises, or when her father shows up. They're at his mercy.

The pecking order is about who eats first. Who's strong, who's weak.

5. Ruffled Feathers

Can she explain this to her kids? No, certainly not. She could stay at the metaphorical level: ruffled feathers a loss of composure, being flustered, embarrassed. But the point of the lessons is origin, how figures of speech derive from real life.

She's seen it many times. The rooster attacks from nowhere, jumping on the hen. She flattens under his weight, sometimes squawking. A quick moment, and it's over. Her feathers behind are a mess.

Rae-Ann trembles to think of it: sneaking around behind the stage that first time, not meaning to, but not resisting. And then finding more places, daring each other to locate dark corners and closets. The thrill of danger, and secrecy. She flushes, remembering how she was smoothing her hair as they left the gym early one morning; how he tugged at his clothes. How the caretaker summed them up in a single glance as he appeared in the hallway, slowly pushing his floor-polishing machine.

6. Henpecked

After her lesson-filled night, Rae-Ann arrived at school pouch-eyed, planning to cut ties to Rick. The hardest thing would be working with him. Only two months until summer vacation. She could hang on.

She threaded her car through the parking lot—late again, school buses arriving. Gathering her bags, she failed to see Sue standing by the car. She pushed the door open, almost hitting her, and then toppled back into the driver seat.

"Sorry! I didn't realize—"

"Come with me." Sue walked toward the school, not waiting.

"What's going on? What about my class—?"

"You should have thought of that before."

She took a seat in the principal's office. Behind the desk, Sue fired each word with extra space in between. She was quivering: something big happening, and she wasn't sorry. When had she begun to dislike Rae-Ann so much?

Only a few phrases pierced her consciousness: shocking behaviour, suspension until the hearing, union informed.

"Do you have anything to say?" Sue sat forward, fingers spread across the desktop.

Rae-Ann gripped her knees and leaned over as though trying to stop a nosebleed. A disciplinary hearing for *her*: that was rich. Discipline was what the overfed, overscheduled, overpraised students needed instead of parents who indulged every passing desire and argued with teachers every day of the week. She snorted, clapping a hand over her mouth, and struggled to sit up straight and speak calmly.

"Where's Rick?"

"I'm not at liberty to discuss other employees."

So he wasn't getting suspended. No discipline for him. She was the easy target; he'd work the system, dodge and deny.

She tilted her head toward the desk, looking at the floor. Sue flipped a pencil between her fingers. There was a lot of traffic in the main office, just outside Sue's door. Rae-Ann glimpsed more than one teacher bustling around the copier. The door open for maximum humiliation. Her skin tingled and tightened with heat as she realized that everyone must know about her and Rick, that they'd known all along.

"Listen, I'll admit I'm disappointed. Absolutely, profoundly disappointed. I thought you were a good teacher. Too smart to carry on like this with a married man. And at your own school, of all places."

"What did you say?"

"You heard me—" The pencil flew across the room, clattering. "Oh, come on. Don't tell me that's news."

She stared at the framed graduation certificates on the wall behind Sue, willing herself not to break down before she could get off school property.

Sue clasped her hands together, working them, and sighed heavily, shaking her head several times. She said, "Oh, dear."

They sat in silence while Sue shuffled papers.

Finally: "I am a good teacher."

"I'll walk you to your car."

Henpecked: often misapplied to husbands. Excited by weakness, hens will peck an injured sister, drawing blood, until death.

7. Playing Chicken

Soon after they feather out, young chickens challenge each other, hopping higher, brandishing wingspan, and staring each other down. Human variations exist. In the swimming pool, friends ride on each other's shoulders, wrestling until someone is pushed off, shrieking and splashing. On the road, two cars approach each other in the same lane until one finally swerves. And in love, a woman can fight back, if she gathers strength. There's a wife—a wife!—who would benefit from knowing more about her husband. There's a union to press Rae-Ann's cause. The steward she'd spoken with had mentioned workplace harassment. Tentatively, with a question in his voice—had she thought of it? Well, no, she hadn't. So, what did that make her: cheap, naïve, clueless, or harassed? Her fault or not her fault? She's wounded now, too stunned to know. But later, these are possibilities: the wife and the union. Can she play the game? Who will blink first?

When you play chicken, there is only one winner.

8. Fox in the Henhouse

This farmyard predator is sneaky, but its behaviour is predictable. It occurs to Rae-Ann, as she ponders her life from inside the coop, that she might also construct a series of lessons around foxes, starting with fairy tales. In terms of poultry, though, it's accurate to say that a fox will take a hen cleanly, without trailing any feathers. It chooses, excises, leaves, and later comes back for more.

The proverbial fox is harder to identify. Rick in the staffroom could qualify. So could she, carrying her penknife. But she's not a threat, not really. She intends no harm.

Children, a fox in the henhouse means danger.

9. A Chicken with Its Head …

Her father installed the first chicks when Rae-Ann and her sisters were teenagers, giving them a job to do. Since that time, on reaching maturity, the meat birds have been packed into crates and sent away for processing, coming home in plastic bags. Laying birds can stay as long as they're productive.

While they've never done the slaughtering themselves, Rae-Ann thinks of an easy twist of the neck, quick and painless. She could manage it. There's something essential about blood, though. She'll have to cut it. A dramatic smear of blood on the wall, a spattering arc as she throws the carcass at him: this will be her statement. Disappointed he may be, but let him also be surprised.

A hen turns its head to look at her, coming closer. She admires its black and white plumage, the red face and comb. Skeletal feet opening and closing, delicate yet strong. She could never hurt this living work of art.

"Thanks for the egg." Rae-Ann raises her hand slowly. The hen skitters away, wings flapping. Leaving her.

Why is she reduced to talking to animals? What is she doing in this stinking prison? Rae-Ann heaves her purse across the coop. It lands in the far nest box with a thunk, striking a sitting hen, which flops to the floor as the other hens squawk and beat their wings, making clouds. She rushes over to the limp bird. It doesn't move. An unrecognizable wail rises, filling the tight space with all her misbegotten impulses and the wretched places they lead her.

The hatch-door opens, but no one appears. "Rae-Ann? Honey?"

His voice a surge of voltage on the line, a connection she didn't expect. She listens, trying to hear over the sound of her harsh, uneven breathing.

"A lady from the school called all worried. Let me help you out of there. Come on into the house."

Gentle. Not criticizing, not demanding.

But who phoned? Not Rick, a woman. The school had the number for next-of-kin emergencies, but she can't imagine Sue or any of them caring enough about her well-being to call. They hate her. Don't they?

Rae-Ann slumps against the wall, squeezing her eyes shut.

"Rae? Do you think you can come out? How about something to eat?"

She opens her eyes, expecting to see his face studying her. But the only part of him that's visible is his hand gripping the edge of the portal to the everyday world. His hand is freckled, like his face. Like her face. Dark hair curls over his fingers; the nail beds are white from holding on so hard. He's straining, staying outside so as not to startle her. Or else he's afraid to look in.

"What about a nice warm bath? How does that sound?"

Beneath the calm words, audible fear. He's afraid what he'll find out about his daughter if he looks into the coop. She's never known him to be afraid of anything.

Rae-Ann pats a cushion of straw around the failing hen, beyond her power to save, and contemplates the terms of her exit. Too many contradictory ideas throng her head. She tries to untangle knowledge and shame, hope and dread and sorrow, and finds that she can't keep any strand separate from the others. If only she had a clear idea of what happens next. But clarity has not come to her in the coop. She'll have to leave without it.

In weeks or months, she might be ready to begin fixing the humiliating damage, if it can be fixed. Right now, the only sure thing is that she's entered a kind of limbo. Home for a rest. Surprised by kindness. Still lost, but also found, and there's nothing in the world of chickens to describe it.

Acknowledgements

I am grateful to Melissa, Sarah, Sharon, and Jamis at Turnstone Press for their support and for the care they took with this book. Many thanks to Patricia Sanders, whose insightful commentary and sure advice made the editing process a pleasure. Thanks to the editors of publications in which my work has appeared, including *The Antigonish Review*, *The Dalhousie Review*, *The Humber Literary Review*, *Kindred*, *The New Quarterly*, *Southword*, and *U of T Magazine*. I especially want to salute *The New Quarterly*'s Susan Scott, Pamela Mulloy, and Kim Jernigan, superwomen.

The communities that writers create keep me going. Deep gratitude to workshop leaders and fellow participants at One Story, Tin House, and Write on the French River, and to Isabel Huggan, my mentor at the Humber School for Writers. Thanks to friends who read early versions of stories, for invaluable comments and support: Michelle Berry, JC Sutcliffe, Charlotte Beck, Frank Vitale, and Cathy Wilson. Jonathan Bennett has sustained my writing in important ways—thank you.

I am grateful to the Ontario Arts Council for Writers' Reserve grants and to the Canada Council for a professional development grant.

Love and gratitude to my parents, Bea Parker and Bill Rock, for their unshakeable belief that a book would appear; and to Mary Rock, Bill Parker, Bill and Jennifer Rock, Tom Rock and Terry Cosentino, Bonnie Gaughan and the Gaughan family.

To Tim, and to our children, Molly, Sarah, Madeleine, and Joseph: all my love. You are light on the journey.